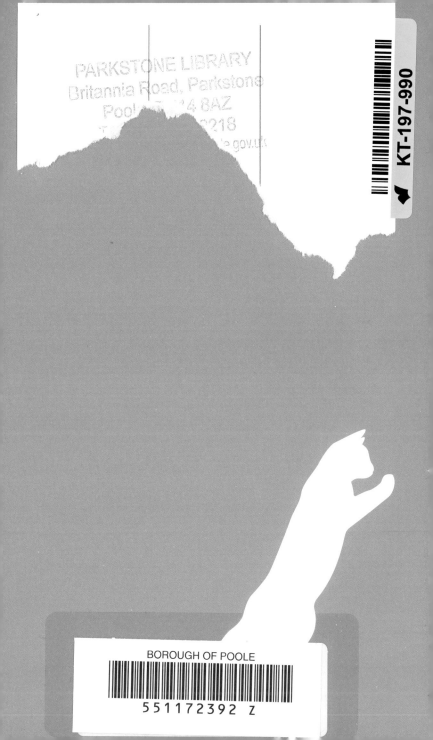

KT-197-990

A Cat Called
ALFIE

Rachel Wells is a mother, writer and cat lover. She lives in Devon with her family and her pets and believes in the magic of animals. Rachel grew up in Devon but lived in London in her twenties working in marketing and living in a tiny flat with an elderly rescued cat, Albert. After having a child she moved back to Devon and decided to take the plunge and juggle motherhood with writing.

She has always wanted to write and found her voice in her first novel, *Alfie the Doorstep Cat* which went on to become a *Sunday Times* bestseller. *A Cat Called Alfie* is her second book.

A Cat Called

ALFIE

Rachel Wells

AVON

A division of HarperCollinsPublishers
77–85 Fulham Palace Road,
London W6 8JB

www.harpercollins.co.uk

A Hardback Original 2015
1

Copyright © Rachel Wells 2015

Rachel Wells asserts the moral right to
be identified as the author of this work

A catalogue record for this book is
available from the British Library

ISBN 978-0-00-814219-3

Set in Bembo by Ben Gardiner

Printed and bound in Great Britain by
Clays Ltd, St Ives plc

MIX
Paper from
responsible sources
FSC C007454

I feel so privileged to have been able to write about Alfie for a second time and there are a lot of people I am indebted to.

Thank you to my editor, Helen Huthwaite, for continuing this journey with me; it has been a pleasure yet again working with you and all the team at Avon. To see how much you care about Alfie is incredibly overwhelming.

I would not have been able to do this without my amazing agents, Kate and Diane, and their team at Diane Banks Associates. Always on hand with the best advice, you had the unenviable job of keeping me sane this year – no easy feat.

My family deserve a round of applause for putting up with me and helping me greatly whenever I needed it. Thom – you've been amazingly cat-knowledgeable; Mum thanks for all the help with Xavier; and Xavier, thanks for letting your mummy write when she needed to. Also to Jo for your amazing support and I love you all so much. Thanks to Helen, Becky, Martin, Jack and family for taking such good care of Xavier while I worked, knowing he has such a loving second family around him is priceless.

Special love to the wonderful women I call my friends, especially Jo, Jas, Tam, Tammy, Tyne, Jessica, Sally and Tina – I adore you all and am blessed to have you in my life. Prosecco all round!

A big nod must also go to Frankie and team at Morans in Westward Ho! It served as the perfect place to write, and provided much needed coffee, delicious food and inspiration – thank you Tomasz!

Alfie is a combination of the cats I have had the good fortune to know and love throughout my life, and therefore he is real to me. I cannot thank enough those who have read and enjoyed the book for embracing this very special cat.

For Xavier - you are my sunshine

-CHAPTER-

One

I yawned and stretched, blinking into the dark night. The sky was clear, stars sprinkled sparsely above me, and the moon lit us up in a spotlight.

'I'd better go home, Tiger,' I reluctantly said. 'They might be worrying.' It wasn't often that I stayed out so late, but Tiger and I had been having fun with some of the neighbourhood cats and I'd lost track of time.

'OK, Alfie, I'll walk you home.' Although Tiger, my best friend, was a girl cat, she was pretty tough and definitely scarier than I was. And, after all I had been through, I quite liked having her as my bodyguard. Even as we strolled down Edgar Road together, passing dark houses, lit street lamps, and parked cars, I jumped occasionally at my shadow. I was a bit nervous in the dark; past memories were conjured up, things I would rather forget, but Tiger was striding protectively next to me so I tried to remember that I was safe now.

'Look, Tiger,' I exclaimed, fear forgotten, as we stopped near the house next door to mine; number 48 Edgar Road.

'My goodness, it looks as if someone is moving in,' she replied.

'At this time of night!' I exclaimed. This was incredibly strange – not only did I know that humans normally slept at night but they also normally moved house during the day.

We snuck into the front garden and hid behind a bush, a place we knew well, as we excitedly watched events unfold.

Tiger and I had staked out this house on many an occasion. In fact we knew it almost as well as we knew our own.

A few months ago the current owners had moved out and a 'To Let' sign had gone up. I'd persuaded Tiger to join me to check out the progress of the house on many occasions; even after all this time, I couldn't resist the lure of an empty home. A few years ago, having found myself homeless, I was taught by a wise cat that empty houses heralded new people, and therefore potential families for cats in need. Like a moth to a flame, they called me to them. Although I now had loving families, and I certainly wasn't a cat in need, I still found myself drawn to them.

There was a large white van parked outside and two men were unloading it. Both men were wearing jeans and jumpers; one wore a woolly hat, the other had very little hair. They were both tall; one was slim, the other a bit more rotund. They were largely silent as they carried large boxes from the van and into the house.

I purred with excitement.

'New owners! I can't wait to meet them,' I said to Tiger.

'Oh, Alfie, you're such a doorstep cat. When it comes to new families, you just can't help yourself can you?' Tiger asked. I shook my head. 'You don't think it's odd?' she added.

'Well yes a bit,' I replied.

'Who moves stuff into a house in the middle of the night?'

She was right, I thought, as I pondered why on earth they would choose the dead of night to move their belongings in?

When I first arrived at Edgar Road, over three years ago now, I had been taught that the signs they put up outside houses signalled that new people were moving in. I had arrived in the street homeless, abandoned after my owner passed away. Scared, lonely and with nowhere to go, I had used those signs to find the four houses that would soon become my new homes.

Without realizing it, I had become a doorstep cat; a cat who visits or lives in multiple houses. With so many homes, I could ensure that I was always going to be fed and loved. Finding myself totally alone in the world, without an owner, had broken my heart and I knew I could never face that again.

I had started with four new homes in Edgar Road, but they had dwindled to two after families had moved. So although I was pretty secure, I found old habits hard to break, and couldn't help investigating empty houses. You never knew what was around the corner.

'It's a fairly big house,' Tiger pointed out. 'Which probably means a whole family will move in.' Tiger lived only a few doors down from me but her house was smaller. My main family, Jonathan and Claire, were now married after I had brought them together, and lived in Jonathan's large house, which cried out for a family. It was too big for just two people and a cat; it badly needed children running around it. They both wanted one, or maybe more than one, but I was their spoilt baby for now. Not something you would ever hear me complain about.

'I hope there'll be a big family moving in, with some nice children. But I hope they don't have a cat.'

'Why?'

'Well, I was hoping that this new family might need a doorstep cat.'

Tiger lay down in the bush, looking pensive.

'You've got Jonathan and Claire, and Polly and Matt now. Don't you think that it's time to accept that you have families who love you and you don't need to look for any more homes?' Tiger yawned, a long lazy yawn; lecturing me always seemed to take it out of her.

I knew in my little heart that what she was saying was true, but knowing something and feeling it were two completely different things.

We watched as the men took the last of the boxes out of the van, and then shut the door. They took them into the house, emerging again a few minutes later.

'I really don't know how to thank you,' the slim man said. He looked sad. I had crept closer, so I could hear more clearly.

'Hey, don't worry about it. That's what family's for,' the other one replied, patting him on the back.

'I know but, well, where we are now, what's happened, I just don't know how to—' His voice broke with emotion; my eyes widened.

'That's it then?' The other man changed the subject.

'Yup. That's pretty much everything we own, done now.' He laughed bitterly.

'Come on, little brother, it'll be fine,' the first man said.

'I wish I could believe you,' he replied, as they got into the van and drove off.

'Wow, now I am definitely intrigued,' I mused, as we watched them go.

'Alfie, I really think it's time to give up looking for new homes,' Tiger stated with another yawn. I looked over at her and realized it was definitely time for bed. Tiger might be a young cat like me, but boy did she need her sleep.

'You're right, I'm sure,' I agreed, 'but then, once a doorstep cat always a doorstep cat.'

-CHAPTER-
Two

My house was in darkness as I jumped through the cat flap. I wasn't surprised, it was late. I lapped up some water, before taking myself off to my cat bed, upstairs on the landing.

After Claire and Jonathan first got together, I was still splitting my time between their two houses and the other two flats. I took credit for their relationship as I introduced them. It was funny; I had been planning to do so but it actually happened unwittingly. When I was injured and recovering at the vet, Jonathan went looking for me, and Claire realized I was his cat too. They fell in love, being perfect for each other, and were together for six months before Claire and I moved into Jonathan's house. A year later they got married. It was my first experience of a human wedding. I was even part of the ceremony, which was held in a small church not far from Edgar Road. I was so excited until they put a lead on me – oh the indignity! – but I forgave them because they included me in their special day, plus they gave me pilchards to eat. Yum. I stayed with my other family, Polly, Matt, Henry and their new baby, Martha, while they went on what they called a 'honeymoon', but now I lived with Jonathan and Claire almost full time.

As I lay in my bed, thinking about the new family, I was unable to figure out why on earth anyone would move boxes in the middle of the night. I also couldn't stop thinking about how upset the man seemed. He definitely sounded like a human in need from my experience; someone who could clearly do with my help. I was still fretting over it as I fell asleep.

★★★

I woke the following morning later than usual. I had a good long stretch, and then made my way to Claire and Jonathan's room where they were still asleep. It was the weekend, so they didn't have to get up early. However, I was hungry and it was definitely past my usual breakfast time. Luckily they hadn't fully shut the bedroom door so I pushed it open.

I jumped up onto the bed, climbed onto Claire's chest and miaowed loudly.

'Arggh, Alfie,' Claire started as she sat up and found me sitting on her. 'Why do you always sit on me and not him?' she asked, gesturing to Jonathan who was clearly pretending to still be asleep.

I miaowed to say that I sat on her because Jonathan could be really grumpy in the morning; Claire was a better bet.

'I get it,' she continued. 'It's breakfast time.' She got up and pulled her dressing gown off the chair next to the bed and put it on.

'And while you're up, coffee would be great,' Jonathan said, still refusing to open both eyes. I stood over him on the bed, tickling his cheek with my tail until he was forced to open his eyes and sit up. 'Get off me, Alfie, I can't bear it,' he said, stroking me, but at the same time gently pushing me away.

'Good one, Alfie,' Claire said, giggling. She picked me up, tucked me under one arm and carried me downstairs with her.

'Claire, Claire.' Jonathan appeared, breathless some time later. 'Have you seen my trainers?' he asked, stopping to bend down to stroke me. I had finished my breakfast and licked myself clean by the time he appeared.

'In the cupboard under the stairs, where we keep all the

shoes,' she replied with a tut. Claire was incredibly tidy; the house was always immaculate, yet still Jonathan couldn't seem to find anything. Claire said it was a 'man thing', although that certainly didn't apply to me. Luckily I was a very clean and tidy cat who appreciated order, so we all lived well together.

'I'll have another look, you know how hopeless I am.' He kissed her. It was one of those long kisses you see in films, and I felt as if I was intruding a bit as I covered my eyes with my paws. As I uncovered them, he pinched her bottom and went off again to search for the elusive trainers. Claire's face was pink with happiness and every time I saw her like that I remembered why I had wanted them to be together in the first place. It wasn't perfect – I had learnt that perfect relation-ships rarely existed, either for cats or humans – but Jonathan and Claire made each other happy nearly all the time and we had a sunny, loving home. Tiger was right, I was lucky with the life I had and sometimes I really needed to remember that.

'Found them!' Jonathan came back into the kitchen look-ing triumphant, brandishing his trainers. 'Right, darling, I'll go to the gym then we can go out for lunch when I get back?'

'Lovely, and I'll put my feet up until you get back,' she said, hugging him. 'By the way, you do know what today is, don't you?'

'Um, Saturday?' Jonathan replied.

'You know what I mean,' Claire said in a very quiet voice. Not that she needed to whisper as I had no idea what that meant.

'I hadn't forgotten, my love.' He smiled and kissed her cheek. 'I'll see you later.' I noticed him wink before he left.

Humans, I often say, are funny creatures. I love them very much and they take good care of me, but I don't suppose I will ever fully figure them out. Take Jonathan and his trainers. He knows where they're kept but he opens the cupboard, doesn't see them, asks Claire, and then finds them where he looked in the first place. Jonathan does it with everything and for some reason Claire seems to find it funny and endearing, whereas I think it's annoying. It's not like he's stupid but he definitely acts as if he is sometimes.

And Claire, she whispers a lot in front of me, although she doesn't know just how much I actually understand. Which is quite a lot. I'm pretty sure when she speaks softly like that, it's because they are trying to have a baby. I know what a baby is; I've had experience with Henry and Martha who live down the road. Plus, we cats quite like babies – they are small and warm and a bit like us in some ways.

But they haven't got pregnant yet. I know it makes Claire upset sometimes and I worry because she was sad a lot of the time when I first knew her and although she seems happy life is unpredictable, and things can change in the flick of a switch.

A little while after Jonathan had left, the doorbell rang out and I rushed to the front door with Claire. She opened it to find Polly, from my other home, standing on the doorstep with a beautiful smile on her face. Claire and Polly were close friends now, and I'd brought them together too.

'Hi.' Claire beamed back at her. I purred and went to greet Polly. When I first met her she never smiled, but now she did all the time. She was so beautiful that she lit up everyone with her smile, even me. All my humans were attractive in their own ways but Polly was stunning. Everyone agreed but Polly laughed it off and was probably the least vain person I knew – she was certainly less concerned with her appearance than I was with mine.

'Hope you don't mind me popping in but you said that Jon was going to the gym. Matt's just taken the kids to the park so I've managed to escape.'

'Don't be silly, of course I don't mind, come in.' Claire stood aside.

'Hi, Alfie.' Polly bent down to pet me. She and I were good friends now; we had come a long way since we first met.

Claire made a pot of coffee and as they settled round the kitchen table, I manoeuvred myself to sit at Polly's feet, casually brushing my tail against her legs.

'I'm not sure I should be drinking coffee,' Claire said, taking a sip.

'Are you?' Polly asked.

'No, I'm not pregnant but I am ovulating.'

'Take my advice, hon, just try to relax. I was drinking more than just coffee when I got pregnant with both of mine. Don't put pressure on it, don't make it too much of a thing.' Polly looked concerned, so I rubbed against her legs.

'I try to tell myself that. But you know what I'm like, I get overwrought; I worry about everything. I'm worried that since we've decided to have a baby it'll consume me until it happens.' Claire looked pensive. I also felt bothered about it; she was an anxious person and that's why my getting her and Jonathan together had been a genius move on my part. Jonathan was a complex man – much like myself in many ways – but he treated Claire well. He was old fashioned in some respects and took care of her, at the same time letting her take care of the home, which she seemed to like. I didn't fully understand it, being a cat, but I was learning. Jonathan was like a strong man who kept Claire from being too nervous and sad and she felt safe with him. He could be grumpy but he had a heart of gold and he was loyal to her. Loyalty is so important, I had discovered.

'And that's totally normal, although I really think you need to not let it take over. I mean look at all those unwanted pregnancies. I'm sure it's because the girls don't think about babies that they get knocked up.' Polly laughed.

'I can't stop myself now, though.' Claire smiled. 'Although you're right, I do need to relax.' Claire went to the cupboard and pulled out a biscuit tin that she put on the table.

'So what does Jonathan think?' Polly asked, as she munched on a biscuit.

'He thinks we should just enjoy trying and make the most of it, typical man.' Claire smiled.

'Then, try to do that. He's right.'

'I know, but unlike me Jon is all huff and puff; he's got a short temper but then he's able to let things go easily, he doesn't stew on things thank goodness. I think he'll make a good dad.'

Polly reached over and gave Claire's hand a squeeze.

'You'll both make great parents, better than me anyway,' she said with a sad smile.

'Come on, Pol, when are you going to forgive yourself?' Claire asked.

When I first met Polly she was in a bad way. It was discovered that she had post-natal depression which means you are sad after having a baby, and in a way I was responsible for her getting help. Henry was a happy, healthy baby and now he was a very contented little boy but it took a while before Polly got better. When she had baby Martha just over a year ago, she had been terrified that she would feel that way again, but thankfully she didn't. They are now a happy family and I love having Henry and Martha as my playmates.

'I don't think I ever will. I know, deep down, it wasn't my fault, but because everything was so good with Martha I guess I'll always feel guilty about Henry. Anyway, that's just something that I'll have to accept; but you don't need to worry about that.' Polly looked pensive.

'No, I am going to have enough trouble worrying about not getting pregnant.' Claire paused. 'My friend Tasha is having acupuncture.'

'Ouch.'

'Well she swears it doesn't hurt. She and her boyfriend have been trying a while, and I'm kind of toying with giving it a go. It's just Jon worries that the more I do to get pregnant the more of a state I'll get into, like a vicious circle.'

'I agree, and I couldn't do it, I hate needles.' Polly shuddered.

Claire poured more coffee and as I slid into a half-dozing state, they chatted about work and the house, the topic of babies safely abandoned.

'Anyway, lovely, I better go, and make them all some lunch,' Polly said as they finished their drinks. 'But remember Franceska and the boys are coming over tomorrow. They want to see Alfie.'

I opened my eyes and miaowed loudly to say I wanted to see them too.

'I swear that cat understands everything we say,' Claire said, picking me up so we could both see Polly to the door.

Goodness, I loved my humans but they weren't always very clever. Of course I could. I understood nearly everything anyway.

-CHAPTER-

Three

Despite Tiger's best efforts, I was loath to go for our usual morning constitutional in case I missed a minute with Aleksy and little Tomasz. Aleksy was my first child friend ever; I met him when he moved to Edgar Road, and he and I had an unshakable bond as a result. Although I was fond of his younger brother, Tomasz – who confusingly had the same name as his dad – and of course Henry and Martha, Aleksy was my best child friend.

'We can watch the empty house,' I suggested to Tiger. It was close enough to Polly's for me to keep an eye on both, and watch for the arrival of Aleksy. Since the activity on Friday night there had been nothing more happening, which made the empty house even more mysterious. Still no one seemed to live there.

'Alfie, nothing is happening. I might go and see what the other cats on the street are doing,' Tiger said huffily. I looked at her, with my most charming expression, but she wouldn't look at me.

'Women', I thought to myself, an expression I had learnt from Jonathan.

'OK, but we can play later,' I suggested, still trying to placate her, but she stalked off. I knew she would sulk for a while but then she'd forget to be angry. Tiger didn't hold grudges; that was why we remained good friends, but she could be temperamental. I had heard Jonathan saying that most women were, and Claire always shouted at him when he said that, so I am pretty sure he is right.

★★★

I padded around the front garden of the empty house on my own. The people who lived there previously were a house share; five young professionals – that was how Claire described them. Although they were nice enough they were barely there and had no interest in cats, so I was unfamiliar with the house.

There was no sign of anyone and, apart from the boxes and furniture, the house was still puzzlingly empty. I still hadn't been able to figure out why they would have moved their stuff in, in the middle of the night, and not themselves. It made no sense. A mystery. I jumped up onto a low windowsill of a front room to make sure, but nothing had changed. As I jumped down I let my mind wander again, thinking about who might soon be living there. I imagined a lovely family, older children maybe, as I didn't have any of them in my life. Hopefully they would be fish-lovers too (eating not keeping), so I would get plenty of treats. And I prayed that there would be absolutely, definitely no dogs.

I smiled to myself as I left the front garden and walked up the road to Polly's house. When I first met Polly and Matt they lived in a flat but now they had a house. It was a lovely, cosy home. Polly had put a lot of work into the decor, and there were lots of pictures, photos and vibrant cushions in the living room. It made it very comfortable when I visited, and they even had a cat bed for me. After all, it was my second home.

I stood at the front door. I could have gone around the back to where they had put in a cat flap, but I wanted to greet Aleksy the minute he arrived. My little legs were almost shaking with excitement as I waited. The weather wasn't too bad; it was warmish and there were glimpses of sun for me to bask in. I also spent a bit of time smelling the flowers that Polly had planted, lots of red, yellow and orange coloured buds. I was careful not to get too close; last year Tiger put her nose into a flower and had been stung by a bee. She had to go to the vet and was in a lot of pain, and then had to have a nasty injection. There was no way I wanted that to happen to me. After carefully sniffing from a safe distance, I lay down in a patch of sunlight, to sunbathe.

'Alfie,' a familiar voice said a little while later. I opened my eyes. Aleksy was standing over me, smiling. He looked such a big boy now – he'd recently had his seventh birthday – in his jeans and sweatshirt. He had been in England for three years and although I still knew little about Poland where they had come from, he seemed to be becoming more and more English every time I saw him.

I stood up and purred in greeting. Aleksy picked me up and I nestled into his neck. Little Tomasz stroked me and I purred at him to let him know how pleased I was to see him as well.

'Right, boys, let's go in, including you, Alfie,' Franceska, the boys' mum said, leaning down to stroke me. Franceska was a lovely calm lady and had worked very hard to help her family settle in England. Although she had served in a shop for a while, she now worked with her husband, big Tomasz, in his restaurant when her boys were at school. I had never been there, it was quite far from Edgar Road for a cat to venture, but I had heard from my families that it was pretty good, popular and they were doing well. I actually wished I could go and visit them, just to see where they lived. The family now lived in a flat over the restaurant and I missed them. When they lived on Edgar Road, I used to see Aleksy almost every day and now we only saw each other once a week.

We were all in Polly's warm front room. Martha was holding onto the dark blue sofa – she was learning to walk. I had learnt that whilst cats walk from birth, it takes humans longer, which is another thing that makes me wonder why they say that humans are cleverer than cats. I can think of many reasons why it's the other way round, and not just the walking thing.

Henry and Tomasz immediately started playing with Henry's train set. Tomasz was older than Henry but they played together well. I know Aleksy often said that he was too big to play with the younger boys but I could sometimes tell that he wished he could join in. Instead he played with me. He always kept toys for me and brought them over when he came. He took them out of his backpack now and although I often felt such playing was a bit beneath me, at six cat years, I indulged him and let him dangle a fake mouse, roll a ball and I even chased the ribbons and bells. It amused Martha anyway, who was trying to balance and grab my tail at the same time. I dodged easily, but knew if she kept trying it wouldn't end well for her.

When Polly and Franceska returned from the kitchen, they had a tray with hot drinks for the grown-ups, squash for the children and a plate of biscuits. Immediately the boys descended on the biscuits.

'Only one each,' Franceska said, but I saw Aleksy take two with a grin.

Polly picked up Martha to give her a bottle of milk and when I miaowed, to say that I felt left out, Polly grinned.

'Frankie, can you get Alfie some milk? He obviously wants a snack too.' I followed Franceska to the kitchen and lapped up the milk when it was presented to me. Aleksy followed me in and we found ourselves alone. The kitchen had a small round table and four chairs on one side, in the dining area, and was fitted with grey wooden cupboards on the other. I don't know much about interior design being a cat and only having a basket to call my own, but Polly definitely had a flair, because her home looked a bit like she did, as if it came from one of those glossy magazines that Claire liked to read. In fact, Claire was talking about getting her to help redecorate our house.

'I miss you, Alfie,' Aleksy said as I finished my milk. I looked at him, as I cleaned myself up, trying to read his eyes and my heart sank. I could see it, sadness in his little face, and it caused me physical pain. I was always greatly affected by the emotions of my humans but the children, especially Aleksy, were the worst. I rubbed myself against his legs to tell him I missed him too. 'Sometimes I think we should still live here when I could see you every day,' he said. I purred in concurrence.

'Aleksy.' Tomasz ran into the kitchen like the whirlwind he was. Aleksy was the sensitive child whereas little Tomasz was more physical.

'What, Tommy?' Aleksy asked.

'Claire is here and she bought us a present.' Tomasz shook with excitement and Aleksy's eyes lit up as he ran into the living room.

Whatever was bothering Aleksy would obviously have to wait.

'Alfie.' Claire scooped me up. 'I was looking for you. I swear this cat is still as elusive as ever, I sometimes wonder if he's found other homes.'

'Surely not?' Franceska said.

'Well, he's always out and about. Who knows? He stays with us most nights but …'

'Well he visits us most days,' Polly pointed out.

I miaowed loudly. I might be curious about the residents moving into the new house, but I knew who my families were.

As I snuggled on Franceska's lap I surveyed the living room with a swelling heart. The boys were all playing a game that Claire had bought them. Martha had fallen asleep, curled up beside Polly on the sofa, her chubby legs sticking out from a blanket. Claire was animated, Franceska stroked me as she listened and chatted, and Polly was smiling. I was such a lucky cat, I really was. My last thought, as like Martha, I took my nap, was how happy I felt to see love, happiness and my families in that room.

CHAPTER
Four

I was washing myself in the kitchen after breakfast when the cat flap clanged and Tiger breathlessly appeared. We often went into each other's homes, but we had to be careful that our owners didn't catch us as they could be a bit mean to uninvited cats. But Tiger knew that Jonathan and Claire were at work on a weekday, so she was safe.

'What are you doing?' Tiger asked. She sounded excited.

'I was about to go to Polly's. She normally takes a walk to the park, so I thought I might tag along.'

'Well, you might want to come with me instead.' She made it sound like a command rather than an invitation.

I followed her out. She jumped onto the fence in the back garden, then stopped and looked at me.

'Are you OK to jump today?' I looked back at her. My leg was feeling fine today, and I told Tiger so as I followed her.

I had been injured a couple of years ago, when Claire's ex-boyfriend had attacked me. Although my back leg was all right now, some days it hurt more than others, and I knew better than to jump too much in general. It reminded me of what I had been through; like a deep-rooted scar. I'd been lucky to survive but I didn't want to think about that right now.

More important things were a-paw.

I still didn't know what was going on until Tiger led me into the back garden of number 48, to the patio doors where we could see into the house. We were staring at a kitchen/ dining room like Jonathan and Claire's. And today, we could see that the boxes had been unpacked.

'I didn't see any people yesterday, did they come this morning?' I asked.

'No, which is why I had to come and find you. I got up really early, and when I walked past the front of the house I saw that the living room boxes had been unpacked. I checked around before coming to see you but there's no sign of any humans.'

Tiger used to do very little with her time before we became friends. Previously, I had often accused her of being a lazy cat. She had middle-aged owners who indulged her, and who didn't have children so she was spoilt and liked her home comforts. Not that I could blame her for that, as I too used to be a lap cat when I lived with my first owner. However, my good influence was clearly rubbing off on her and since we'd been friends, she had become a bit more adventurous.

'Let's see if we can find the others and see if they know anything,' I suggested. So we ran to the end of the street where we found some of our friends hanging out.

When I was attacked by Claire's ex-boyfriend Joe, Tiger had told all the other cats how I had provoked Joe in order to save Claire from a relationship with him; a man who turned out to be a horrible bully. My plan worked a treat, despite the fact I nearly died, but after I recovered I found myself a bit of a hero among the local cats. Even Tom, who could be quite mean, showed me a grudging respect and no longer tried to fight me. I finally had cat friends who were ready to look out for me, after such a long time of feeling alone in the world.

Elvis, Nellie and Rocky all greeted us warmly.

'Do you know anything about number forty-eight?' I asked.

'I do, actually,' Nellie announced sounding smug.

'Well what is it?' I asked.

'Last night it was very late, there were no lights on in any of the houses, only the street lamps. Anyway I was taking a bit of a stroll with Ronnie.' Ronnie was another of our cat friends, but Ronnie was almost completely nocturnal and I never saw her during the day.

'Go on,' I encouraged. The problem with Nellie was that she liked a drama.

'I'm getting to it. Anyway, we were strolling, but a car pulled up, as I said it was the middle of the night.'

'Get on with it.' Tiger scowled.

'OK, keep your fur on. Anyway, so the car pulled up and two men got out. I guess they were unpacking but after a couple of hours, they got back in the car and left.'

'Right, so what did the men look like?' I asked.

'Just two typical humans, one thin with very little hair whilst the other was fatter with grey-ish hair but that's all I can tell you.' It sounded like the men from the other night.

'So as far as we know no one's moved in there yet?'

'Nope, they left. But it means someone will soon.'

'Yeah thanks, Nellie, we got that,' Tiger finished, giving Nellie a withering look.

'You could always ask, you know, *him*,' Elvis suggested. We all balked at the idea; although Elvis hadn't mentioned his name we all knew which cat he was referring to. And this cat was not one of our friends.

'Oh God, you could but really do you want to?' Rocky asked.

'It's a last resort,' I replied.

'Very last resort,' Tiger concurred. We all shuddered.

As if summoned by magic, the cat in question rounded the corner and made his way towards us. We all grouped together as Salmon approached. He was an unpleasant cat who lived with his owners, Vic and Heather Goodwin, Edgar Road's busybodies. Salmon was as nosey as his owners and also very arrogant, and they lived almost opposite the empty house. He was a fat brown cat with mean eyes; none of us cats liked him and always tried to avoid him if we could. He was known for being a bit of a bully.

'What are you doing?' Salmon asked, narrowing his eyes at us.

'We were just having a chat,' Tiger replied, staring at him. She was the least afraid of Salmon. Nellie was almost hiding behind Elvis and Rocky looked as if he wanted to run away. Even I felt a bit uneasy as Salmon bared his sharp teeth.

'We were talking about the new people at number forty-eight,' I explained, trying to feel in control.

'Oh well, that's boring,' Salmon said nastily.

'Only because you don't know anything,' Tiger spat back. I admired her bullishness at times.

'If I did, I wouldn't tell you,' Salmon huffed then, hissing nastily at us, he stalked off.

'I hate that cat,' Tiger said. We all silently agreed as we spent the afternoon chasing birds, in order to forget the unpleasantness.

I met Jonathan at the front door as I made it home. I was pleased my timing was so good, as I was pretty hungry after my day's activities. I didn't go into being a doorstep cat to be greedily eating all the time, but at the same time I did enjoy my food. What cat didn't?

'Hi, mate,' Jonathan said, and I rubbed against his suit trousers, which I knew used to annoy him – apparently I left hair behind – but he was more tolerant with me these days. It had only taken three years. 'Coming in for dinner? I've got you some fresh sardines from the deli, but don't tell Claire. Luckily she's at her book club, so it's boys' night in.'

I miaowed as I followed him into the house. This was a good result. A perfect result in actual fact.

Jonathan tipped my dinner into a bowl for me and then he went upstairs to take a shower. While Claire favoured packets of 'cat' food, Jonathan always gave me a finer dining experience. They disagreed about it but on this issue neither of them would budge. I obviously preferred it when Jonathan fed me but I still loved Claire so I tried to be grateful at the ready meals she provided for me. I didn't want to look as though I expected fine dining but I certainly wasn't going to turn it down.

When he came back downstairs, Jonathan was wearing his casual clothes – a T-shirt and jogging bottoms. He grabbed a beer out of the fridge and went into the living room flicking the TV on as he sank down onto the sofa. Jonathan and Claire were so different; he couldn't be in the living room, without the TV being on, whereas Claire would often sit with a book rather than watch the square screen. I followed him in, licking myself clean after my delicious meal. Whilst Jonathan was flicking the TV channels, the doorbell chimed. As Jonathan went to open the door, I followed and was delighted to see Matt on the doorstep holding a pack of beers. Matt was Polly's husband, a tall, quite handsome and very kind man. He and Jonathan had become good friends since my incident and the four of them often spent time together. I was often referred to as Cupid cat, as well as a cat who created friendships. It was a very good thing.

'Free pass?' Jonathan asked him, his voice slightly teasing.

'Polly's putting the children to bed, so I thought I'd see if you fancied a beer? And of course, the football's on in a bit.'

'Excellent. Come in.'

As Matt petted me I congratulated myself on having done good work in bringing friendships together, and maybe when the family moved into number 48, they could become part of our little world too.

I often hear people talking about love, family, relationships and friendships and when you see them working in real life you realize how much of human life hinges on other people. It's not always a good thing though. People can make others happy but they can also make them sad. It is a very complicated concept to unravel. It's different for cats of course, and sometimes people say cats are very self-sufficient, although most of us like being taken care of too.

'So how's work?' Jonathan asked Matt.

'Pretty good, busy but I'm working from home a bit more so I can help Pol out. What about you?'

'You know I was so sceptical when I got my job. I thought the company was a bit rubbish, I thought it was beneath me. But it turns out to be the best move I ever made. Once I got over myself and threw myself into it, it's all started going really well.'

'Finally, it seems that life is good. So let's drink to that.' They clinked beer bottles. 'Oh and by the way, mate, can you and Claire babysit for us on Saturday? I want to surprise Pol with a nice meal out.'

'Sure, I don't think we've got plans and anyway, it's good practice.'

'She's not is she?'

'No, well I don't think so, not yet, but hopefully soon.' Jonathan sounded unperturbed, unlike Claire, as he discussed the wanted pregnancy.

Our cosy boys' night was soon interrupted by the doorbell again. Jonathan groaned as he got up, and I followed him to the front door. He opened the door, coming face-to-face with Heather and Vic Goodwin, who stood smiling – or rather, grimacing – at him from the doorstep.

'Jonathan, is Claire here?' Vic asked. I looked behind Vic and Heather and saw that Salmon was with them, standing at *my* front gate. He aggressively flicked his tail up, I narrowed my eyes but decided to ignore him. Irritating cat. Mind you, irritating owners. They were older than my owners, both with grey hair. They lived in a smaller house, a bit like Matt and Polly's, on the opposite side of the road to us. They always dressed in a similar way, and today they were both wearing navy blue jumpers with white shirt collars poking out from underneath. Vic was wearing corduroy trousers, Heather a corduroy skirt. I wondered if they were a certain species of humans – none of the couples I knew wore matching clothes.

'Um no, she's at her book club,' Jonathan mumbled nervously, as I saw him move forward to block the door. I knew he didn't want to let them in but I also knew he shouldn't underestimate Vic and Heather.

'Not to worry, we've got you.' Heather grinned and before I knew it, they had managed to get themselves inside the house. My fur stood on end. As they walked into the living room, Jonathan shut the door, looking confused. I stayed at Jonathan's feet as we followed them in.

'Ah, Matt, you're here,' Vic said. 'Good, good. Saves us visiting your house.'

'Hello.' Matt looked at Jonathan with panic in his eyes.

'We are—' Heather paused, sitting down on the sofa. I cowered under a chair and put my paws over my eyes. This wasn't good. She continued, 'Here on Neighbourhood Watch business, of course.'

'Of course.' Jonathan and Matt exchanged another glance. Jonathan was standing up, Matt was on the chair in the corner and Vic and Heather sat together on the sofa.

'So what can we do for you?' Jonathan asked, politely.

'Well, as you know there's been a few changes in the street lately. And now number forty-eight has been let we thought it would be a good time to strategize,' Vic started. I pricked my ears up at the mention of the new house.

'Right, strategize how?' Matt asked.

'Well, as you know, dear, Edgar Road has become quite a community and we want to keep it that way. So we thought that when the new people come into number forty-eight we should hold a meeting, explain to them that it's a community here and how we all look out for each other,' Heather explained.

'Sort of a welcome party?' Matt asked, eyebrow raised.

'Exactly, Matt, exactly,' Vic concurred. 'Start as we mean to go on.'

'I didn't get a welcome party,' Jonathan said grumpily.

'Well you didn't act suspiciously when you moved in, did you?' Vic pointed out.

'What are you talking about?' Matt asked.

'Moving boxes in at night, unpacking at night, it's not exactly normal behaviour is it?' Heather smiled, almost in the same way that Salmon does, baring her teeth. I promptly re-covered my eyes.

'And, I have a friend who lives in a nearby neighbourhood, and a house in their street was let recently,' Vic continued. 'Well about twenty of those *foreign* people moved into the house, and well, we can't have that here.'

Jonathan looked shocked, his brows knotted in confusion.

'What on earth are you talking about? What does that have to do with number forty-eight?' Jonathan asked, sounding horrified.

'The letting agent wouldn't disclose to us who would be moving in, but so far the new occupants have acted suspiciously so we've put two and two together. And this is happening all over London, so we need to be on top of it. You know, as Neighbourhood Watch coordinators and concerned residents.'

'So hang on, we don't even know who's moving in, and yet you're already planning to interrogate them?' Matt sounded annoyed.

'No, that's not what we said. But whoever it is, we thought if we invited them to a meeting immediately they would know how our street works. And, we would like them to explain their nocturnal activities. We have a duty to the residents here to ensure our street stays safe,' Heather explained.

'God, you make it sound like a lynch mob.' Jonathan looked aghast.

'No, absolutely not, of course we don't mean that. But anyway, we wanted to inform you and of course we know that you and your good lady wives will attend and offer the neighbourhood your support.' Vic smiled, but his smile was as sinister as his wife's and his cat's.

'It's just that if there are going to be lots of immigrants moving onto the street we need to show them we won't be messed with. And if it's a normal middle-class family we will welcome them,' Heather explained. 'So we can count on you?'

Jonathan and Matt were speechless as I came out from under the chair, and went and sat on the windowsill. Salmon still sat at the gate, and I flicked my tail up at him through the safety of the window. I saw him hiss at me; I smirked, he couldn't come near me, as I continued to taunt him.

'When is this meeting?' Matt asked.

'We are going to schedule it when the residents of number forty-eight move in. So you'll attend I take it?' Vic said.

'I don't know—' Matt began.

'The thing is—' Jonathan said at the same time.

'Dear boys,' Heather started, sounding even scarier than normal. 'I hope that you care enough about this street to come. I would hate to think that you have no interest in where you live, as would the other residents, I'm sure.'

'Absolutely, dear.' Vic put his arm around Heather. 'Until now we have thought of you as being very good members of our community. We wouldn't want to have to revise that opinion.'

Matt looked terrified as he seemed to shrink back into the chair.

'Of course we'll be there,' Jonathan said. Matt shot him a surprised look. 'To welcome our new neighbours, which is, what I hope that this meeting will be about.' Jonathan sounded firm and I was proud of him.

'Absolutely,' Vic said. 'Right, we have lots of people to visit so we'd best get on. Glad we can count on you.' In the whole scheme of Heather and Vic, they'd got off lightly.

'Well good, I'll show you out.' As Jonathan herded them to the door, he spoke again. 'You know our good friends, Franceska and Tomasz are from Poland and they lived here for a while. They weren't trouble makers,' he said. We all stood at the front door; I took the opportunity to give Salmon one last dirty look.

'Absolutely not. We got lucky with them, but not all foreigners are like that,' Heather said, seriously. I could hear Matt in the living room choking on his beer.

'They are unbelievable,' Jonathan said, as he returned to the living room. His face was a bit red, the way it was when he was angry.

'I find them quite amusing. Well apart from the racism of course. You know whenever I walk down the street, I see them over the road, curtains twitching.'

'This will be the lowest crime street ever with those two. Imagine, if they caught you doing anything wrong you'd get talked to death,' Jonathan laughed. 'Or they'd make a citizen's arrest in their matching jumpers.'

'Well, I don't know if it's a family or a hundred immigrants but I already feel sorry for the people moving into number forty-eight,' Matt agreed.

'You're not wrong there. Right, let's forget the Goodwins and put on the football.'

-CHAPTER-
Five

Despite developing a new sleeping habit since Claire and Jonathan moved in together, I had adjusted well to it. Before they were together, when they normally slept alone, they often let me in their room but now, they put my basket on the landing and shut their bedroom door. I wasn't offended; I had since learnt about the human need for privacy when there was more than one of them. And although I didn't understand why I couldn't be in their bedroom, I accepted it. However, I knew instinctively when the alarm clock would go off and as soon as it did I would be waiting to scratch at the door. This delighted Claire who declared me incredibly clever, as I never disturbed them even a minute before the alarm roused them. I have often said that if humans had inbuilt clocks as us cats did, then the world would be a far more efficient place.

Today, I scratched at the door right on cue. It was Jonathan who came to the door first.

'Morning, Alfie,' he said absently, wearing his navy dressing gown. He made straight for the kitchen and his coffee machine. I had learnt that he was a bit of a nightmare in the mornings before he had a cup of coffee. He pulled out cups and I miaowed hopefully.

'OK, hang on, I'll get you some more smoked salmon, but don't tell Claire.' I purred in agreement.

'What are you doing here?' I asked, as Tiger appeared in the kitchen just as I was cleaning myself. 'Claire and Jonathan are getting ready for work, they'll be down any minute,' I hissed.

'Quick, Alfie, I have something to show you.' She looked very pleased with herself; smug even.

'What?'

'Come with me, and you'll see. I have a present for you, a very special present.'

'Wow,' I said as I sat outside number 48 with Tiger. We crept into the front garden, to see if we could get a closer look. Lights were on in the house, we could hear footsteps and when we looked through the window furtively, we saw even more boxes had been unpacked. They had finally moved in. And I fleetingly wondered if our nosey neighbours had been right; they had moved in when no one was around to see them. What was that about?

'I told you, Alfie. They weren't here when I went to bed last night, but when I got up this morning and went for a stroll they were!' She sounded excited.

'They must have come in the night like the boxes,' I mused.

'I guess. Anyway, look.' Tiger led me round the back. We found a bush to hide in, to survey the situation. Through the back patio doors into the kitchen I could see a woman, a bit older than Claire, her hair greying slightly. She was thin and looked harassed as, hair tied back, she was still busily unpacking. After a while she was joined by a man we had seen before; the thin almost bald man. He kissed her and she smiled sadly at him. He was wearing jeans and a shirt and he didn't look as if he was exactly happy either.

'So there's two people?' I asked.

'No, I think there's more. When I came by this morning, I saw someone younger.'

'I'm surprised Salmon isn't here, spying.'

'Thank goodness he isn't. Look!'

I saw a teenage boy enter the kitchen. He was wearing jeans and a hoody and he looked a bit moody. He sat down at the kitchen table, but didn't appear to speak. His mother (I guessed), went over to him and planted a kiss on his head but he acted as if he didn't even notice.

'He doesn't look very nice,' I observed.

'He's a teenager. I think in general they aren't very nice. Well my owners say they aren't. Apparently they are mainly what is wrong with this country.'

'Really?' I hadn't had much experience of teenagers, so I found this fascinating.

'Yes, they are lazy and slovenly and don't care about the world. That's what they say anyway.'

'But you've never had a teenager?' I asked her.

'No, but my family have a couple of friends who have teenage children. They grunt rather than speak and they never say thank you, apparently.'

'Sounds horrible.'

'Yes, but then they grow up and get better, or some of them do.'

'Well that's something, but I'm already dreading the day that Aleksy becomes one.'

'I know, imagine if he's just like that boy there.' We both grimaced.

As we looked, a very pretty blonde girl walked into the kitchen. We retreated slightly as she came over to the floor length windows we were looking through. She looked older than the surly boy, so perhaps she had outgrown this teenage thing. She was tall, taller than her mum, but shorter than her dad. She had beautiful blue eyes but when I looked properly there was something missing from them; she looked distant as she stood in her new home and I had seen that look before. More than once.

What was it with Edgar Road?

After a little while, Tiger got bored and started trying to pull leaves off a bush, but I was mesmerized by the house. People called houses homes but I also thought they were places that contained stories, both happy and sad, and that was what drew me to them.

'Can we go now?' she asked having resorted to looking at her own paw.

'Not yet,' I hissed. 'I just want to see a bit more.'

'Alfie, you and this obsession with humans. Really!' She rolled her eyes as a leaf came loose and landed on her head.

'It's more sensible than your obsession with leaves,' I shot back, staring pointedly at the pile of leaves she'd collected at her feet.

'Is not,' Tiger replied, looking sulky.

'Anyway, we can go soon, I just want to see if it's just the four of them. If it is, then it might not be a bad bet. Another house for me to visit. They might like having a cat around, in any case and there's a nice big kitchen for me to eat in.'

'Oh Alfie, you have enough families who love and take care of you, when will you accept that? And besides, that teenage boy might not like you.' Tiger looked exasperated from having to repeat herself so much.

'My first owner, Margaret, always used to say this thing, Tiger.' I paused as I pictured the kind old lady that I had loved with my whole heart. 'She used to say "We must never rest on our laurels." Now I don't exactly know what it means but I think it means that I shouldn't take *anything* for granted. I once said I would never do that again. And it wouldn't hurt you to take a lesson from me.'

'I'm too lazy. If anything happens to my humans I know you'll sort it out.' She smiled, and of course she was right. It was the sort of cat I was.

A noise startled us.

'Oh my, we hadn't even noticed that,' Tiger said as a cat flap slowly lifted up from the other back door.

'And bang goes my idea of being their doorstep cat,' I murmured, disappointment flooding me. We both stood, stock still as we watched a cat emerge.

'Wow,' I said, unable to contain myself.

'Well,' Tiger said, instantly lost for words.

'Who are you and what are you doing in my garden?' an unfriendly voice hissed and I felt myself glued to the spot as I found myself staring at the most beautiful cat I had ever seen in my life.

CHAPTER
Six

'Who are you?' the beauty hissed angrily at us. I wanted to move, or speak or something but I was rooted to the spot and struck dumb.

'We,' Tiger replied, feistily, 'are your neighbours. I'm Tiger and that's Alfie and we are here to welcome you to Edgar Road.'

I glanced sideways at Tiger, she neither looked nor sounded very welcoming.

'Right, well now you've welcomed me, you may leave.' The exquisite creature stood in front of us. I had never seen such soft fur, bluer eyes or a whiter coat. Her face was like a work of art. She was truly gorgeous, although, admittedly, not at all friendly.

'But we…we…we could show you round,' I stammered, feeling my legs trembling, in an alien sensation.

'Thank you but I think I'll find my own way round. I don't care to ask you again, but would you please get out of my garden.'

'No need to be so rude, whitey,' Tiger hissed. 'We were trying to be friends, but I can see we're wasting our time.'

'Yes you are,' the white cat replied, turning her beautiful back on us and heading back into her house.

'Well, I've never met such a rude cat,' Tiger said as we made to leave.

'I've never met a more beautiful one,' I sighed, stretching my legs out, to try to regain my composure. I had to admit I felt flummoxed. On the one hand, my original idea to become their doorstep cat had been scuppered, but then how could I mind when it had been scuppered by such a beautiful creature?

49

For some reason, the idea of the white cat made me happy and not at all disappointed. In that moment, my aim had changed, rather than be their doorstep cat, I wanted to be the white cat's friend. I was determined to be so.

'Really? You thought she was beautiful? She was horrible, Alfie!' Tiger was angry.

'I didn't think she was nice, just pretty,' I defended myself, but it fell upon deaf ears and Tiger shot me a withering look and stalked off. I followed her but I couldn't get the white cat's image out of my mind.

I trailed behind Tiger as we headed to our little recreation area, where we found four other cats. Elvis, Nellie, Rocky, and mean Tom were all lolling around. Tiger forgot her earlier animosity, eager to tell the others about the new cat. When she had filled them in they turned to me.

'What do you think?' Tom asked, licking his whiskers.

'She's stunning,' I began, but quickly had to duck as Tiger tried to swipe me. 'But yes, definitely rude,' I quickly added. A memory of how Jonathan first was when I met him sprang into my head; he threw me out of his house but he loves me now.

'Well, I wonder if she'll hang out with us.' Nellie interrupted my thoughts.

'I expect, from what we saw she'll keep close to home,' Tiger said, diplomatically.

'I wish *he'd* stay close to home,' Rocky added as Salmon approached.

'I expected to find you here, you are all so boringly predictable. Have you met the new cat?' Salmon asked, in his sneering voice. As much as he disliked us and we disliked him, he couldn't resist trying to find out any gossip.

'Yes,' Tiger replied, refusing to give him more.

'And you think you're so great, but I have met her too,' Salmon said.

'And I bet she wouldn't speak to you,' I added narrowing my eyes at him and feeling braver for some reason.

'Well, no she wouldn't. The silly girl ran away as soon as she saw me.' He sounded annoyed.

'I don't actually blame her for that,' Tiger said. We all laughed. Salmon hissed at her and looked as if he was about to pounce.

'Don't be a silly cat,' Tom said, standing next to Tiger. 'Are you really going to take us all on?' he added.

'You aren't worth it,' Salmon hissed again before turning and stalking off.

'I really dislike that cat,' Rocky stated, echoing all our thoughts.

Wanting to think, I took myself to the little park at the end of the street, leaving Tiger to go home. She said she was tired but I could tell she was still annoyed with me, and off for one of her customary sulks. I tried to give her a friendly nuzzle as we parted but she brushed me off. I thought I would do something nice for her later, even though I wasn't sure exactly what I had done.

When I got to the park I was delighted to see Polly there with the kids. Henry was on the slide and Martha was trying to walk but she kept falling over. I marvelled at her persistence as she kept getting up, with Polly encouraging her.

'Alfie,' Henry shouted, spotting me and running up to me. He knelt down and stroked me and I enjoyed the fuss. I followed him over to where Polly was now carrying a crying Martha.

'Martha, feeling sad?' Henry asked, eyes brimming with concern.

'She bumped herself when she fell over, sweetie,' Polly replied. 'Hi, Alfie.' She smiled at me and I miaowed and put my tail up in greeting.

'Right, well we are going to Franceska's for lunch, although, Alfie, it might be a bit far for you,' she added as she strapped Martha into the buggy and then tried to coax Henry in.

'I walking,' Henry said. And suddenly I had a great idea. I had never been to Franceska's new flat, largely due to my fear of going far from home. When I was forced to leave my first home after Margaret died, I walked for weeks before I got to Edgar Road. I nearly died on a number of occasions – the big roads I had to cross were more dangerous than I could have ever imagined – and so I was fearful, but I did want to see where my third family lived and now, if Henry didn't want to go into the double pushchair then that meant there was a spare seat. I jumped into it.

'Alfie,' Polly admonished. Henry laughed, as did Martha. 'OK, you can come to lunch with us but if Henry needs to go in the buggy you'll have to sit on his lap.' Shaking her head she started pushing us. I looked at Martha who was giving me lots of smiles. I happily flicked my tail; I knew what she meant, this wasn't a bad way to travel.

It seemed quite a long way, and halfway through Henry wanted to get into the pushchair, so Polly put me on his lap.

As we left the quiet of Edgar Road behind, the streets started to get busier, with more shops springing up, more traffic and definitely a lot more people, as Polly manoeuvred the double buggy round them. I soon put my doubts aside and took notice of our route, just in case. We reached Franceska and Tomasz's restaurant, *Ognisko*, where Polly stopped so we could look through the big square window. It looked inviting, I thought, the woodwork on the outside was painted blue, and inside it was full of people, sitting at rustic wooden tables, all looking as if they were enjoying the food that sat on crisp looking linen tablecloths. I was excited to see it for the first time.

We stood next to a different door and Polly rang the buzzer. Franceska opened it with a huge smile, Polly folded the buggy and left it in the entrance as we made our way upstairs to their flat.

'My goodness, you brought Alfie!' Franceska beamed and I grinned back as only a cat can do.

'He jumped into the buggy and so I thought, why not? Although pushing a cat down the road made me feel like a crazy woman.' They both laughed.

'Tomasz?' Henry said, looking for his friend. It always confused me how both father and the younger son of the family were called Tomasz. I called them big Tomasz and little Tomasz to avoid confusion, but it wasn't the most sensible way to name people who lived in the same house.

'Sorry, munchkin, he is at school today and Aleksy too. Come though, you can play with his toys.' Franceska led Henry through to the living room. They had a dining table in the same room as their sofa; it was a big room, warm and inviting and larger than theirs on Edgar Road. The table was laid out with food and I could smell that she had sardines. As if she knew I was coming, my treat awaited. I walked to the table hopefully and miaowed loudly.

'OK, Alfie, you can have your fish. Lucky I had some,

although I had no idea you would be here.' She laughed as she picked me up and gave me a lovely hug.

We spent a lovely afternoon together. I got to explore the flat – it was wonderful to see where they lived. Big Tomasz, Franceska's husband, came up to see us after his lunchtime rush and made a huge fuss of me. Big Tomasz suited the name I gave him; he was a big man who was so much softer than he looked. I always wished I knew him better, but as he worked so much I saw the least of him out of everybody. When we had to leave I felt sad, but on the way back Martha and Henry slept so I curled up on Henry's lap for my lift home, struggling to stay awake after my unexpected excitement.

I jumped out at Claire and Jonathan's and rubbed Polly's legs in thanks for my outing. It was time for me to have a nap but I couldn't resist going to number 48, for one last look. They had already put curtains up at all the windows at the front and the downstairs ones were closed. This was yet another thing that was odd as it was middle of the day. One of the rooms upstairs also had closed curtains.

There was no activity to be seen and no sign of the beautiful white cat. I thought about going round the back but I didn't want to have another run-in until I thought about how best to approach her. For now, I would sleep on it. It was the best solution, I decided, as I made my way round to my back garden. I was about to go through the cat flap when I remembered something. I went over to our garden fence, the one that divided our house from number 48. When I first moved into Jonathan's house, I discovered that one of the panels was a bit loose at the bottom. It allowed me to look through to next door's garden but I hadn't bothered; I had no need to. Until now.

I nudged the panel with my nose and was overjoyed to see that it still moved ever so slightly. It wasn't enough for me to squeeze through but I could see a bit of the garden, I could see the back door too. I could keep an eye on the cat next door, I thought, as I resolved that I would do whatever it took to befriend the white cat. And, as I stepped away from the fence, I knew I wouldn't stop until I succeeded.

CHAPTER
Seven

'I don't mind cooking,' Jonathan offered, as he stood staring at his prized possession, the coffee machine, which was whirring away. When I'd first heard the chrome thing gurgling and spluttering I thought it was alive and would eat me, but now I was used to it. Jonathan liked shiny gadgets that cost a lot of money and made a lot of noise, it seemed.

'Darling, no offence, but when you cook, I have to clean up and it normally takes weeks. Anyway you know what Tasha and Dave are like, they're happy with anything.'

'OK, but if you cook do I have to clear up?'

'Jonathan, stop being an idiot, you know that I clean up as I go along. You can go and get some nice wine, buy some flowers for the house, and treat me to a new dress.'

'Really, all that?' Looking bemused he took his coffee and sat at the kitchen table.

'OK, I don't need a dress but you can get flowers and wine.'

'I would buy you all the dresses in the world if you wanted, you know that.'

'I do and that's why I love you.'

Once again, I had to put my paws over my eyes as they started smooching. I was glad they were happy but I didn't necessarily want to see it. Tasha teased Claire and called it the 'honeymoon period'. I didn't know exactly what it meant but I had guessed that it meant it wouldn't last forever. Hopefully. I was all for affection but people could take it too far – it was almost enough to put me off my breakfast.

It was time for me to leave. I had said I would call on Tiger, so we could hang out. Maybe with some of the others, depending on who was around. For the past few days I had not had a sighting of the beautiful white cat. Or its owners for that matter. And I had spent a fair bit of time at the fence. Not only had I not seen her but I didn't even know her name yet. And I desperately wanted to find out what it was.

I had heard Claire telling Jonathan she had popped round to say welcome, but there had been no answer, although she was sure she'd heard movement in the house. They were certainly mysterious and I wondered if Vic and Heather had managed to get to them yet. They probably had their binoculars trained on the house as it was.

I still hadn't come up with a plan on how to meet the white cat again, but I was working on it. My little brain was always whirring and perhaps today would be the day that I caught sight of her again.

As I made my way out of the back garden – quickly checking the fence for activity – and round to Tiger's house, she was waiting for me, giving herself a clean before we set off for our morning walk.

Exercise was important to me, particularly because of my injury, as I had to keep fit and my limbs moving. So I had taken to going to the park most days, sometimes with Polly, other times with Tiger, as well as strolling up and around Edgar Road.

'Park?' she asked.

'You read my mind,' I replied. The park at the end of our road was small but we loved it. Full of bushes, creatures to chase and, of course, children; we found plenty to entertain us there.

There was also a pond but I didn't like to think about that after a near-death experience I had falling into it once. Matt rescued me but it taught me to keep away from water. I even avoided puddles if I could.

On the way, we sneaked a look at number 48, to see if there had been any developments but nothing had changed. The curtains were drawn, although lights were glimmering through them. I wasn't a judgemental cat but it was most odd.

'Salmon's family said that there might be twenty people living there,' I told Tiger. 'But we only saw four.'

'Yesterday they came round to ours and were ranting on about criminals to my humans. Saying that no one has seen them, they keep the curtains drawn and so they are definitely up to something. They said something about a drugs den but I have no idea what that is.'

'Me neither.' I tried to think about why they might be so secretive. 'But I guess we'll find out soon – they'll have to show their faces at some point.' I was agitated, my excitement at the idea of seeing the white cat again was off the scale. Just then we were rewarded as the front door opened and the surly boy walked out. He looked furtively around and then pulled his hood up as he started walking down the path. I felt all of a quiver as I saw that the cat was at his feet.

'Look, Tiger,' I said, nudging her with my head. We both stood still and looked. When the boy got to the street, he leant down and petted the cat.

'Bye, Snowball,' he said, sounding cross. 'Wish me luck.' Snowball purred and rubbed up against his legs in a most affectionate way. She seemed like a completely different cat from when we met her. And I knew her name!

As the boy walked off she looked directly at us. I gave her

my most charming look but she immediately narrowed her eyes, turned and, with her tail flapping aggressively, stalked back to the front door, where I noticed the woman was standing. She smiled grimly at the cat, picked her up and shut the door.

'Well, I hate to agree with Salmon but they are acting very strangely,' Tiger stated.

'They are, but at least now we know the beautiful cat is called Snowball.'

'Alfie, she's mean! And whilst you may think she's beautiful, I think she's cold.' I raised my whiskers – Tiger sounded cold herself.

'Yes but, Tiger, remember how Jonathan was when I first met him. He was horrid and angry towards me, and now he loves me. I think there's more to this than meets the eye and I intend to find out what's going on.'

'Here we go again,' Tiger said, giving me a stern stare.

I squirmed as I tried to avoid her glaring eyes, but I knew what she meant. I had always meddled and tried to help people; it had been my role since moving to Edgar Road and although things had been calm lately, this little cat couldn't change its fur. Humans often say that curiosity killed the cat but, actually, it was this that kept me going. Part of our intelligence is our interest in everything; that's what I fully believe.

Blip over, we eventually strolled on in companionable silence. Every now and then we'd stop to chase a flying insect, or play with an inviting looking leaf that dangled over the street. I tried to placate Tiger by catching a fly, and I ended up spinning round in circles chasing it, which made her laugh. Soon I was forgiven, although I couldn't help but wonder why she was so grumpy with me recently.

When we got to the park, it was almost deserted. I led Tiger to our favourite area, which had some of the bushiest bushes, as well as lots of colourful flowers and a couple of inviting trees. We played a new favourite game of hiding and then jumping out at each other. Although we were pretty silly, it was enjoyable.

And it was then I saw him.

'Incoming!' I shouted to Tiger, and we scrambled up the nearest tree. A small, rotund dog, with short legs but long hair, yapped up at us as we teased it. When we came here at this time of day we often ran into this particular dog and it had become part of our exercise routine – I had to hide from him when my leg was bad though. The dog was always followed by its screaming owner.

'Roly, come here! Roly, stop, ROLY,' a grey haired woman cried out as she made her way, huffing and puffing over, brandishing a lead as if it was a whip. It made us laugh as she finally clipped the lead on the dog and chastised him.

'Bad dog. We do not chase cats,' she shouted. 'How many times do I have to tell you?'

'Many more, I hope,' Tiger laughed. We weren't in any real danger after all, and it certainly livened up our afternoon.

'Honestly, humans spend all this time and money going to the gym whereas all we have to do is get a dog to chase us,' I observed to Tiger.

'And those humans think they're the smart ones,' she replied with a wry smile.

When we got back to Edgar Road, Tiger went off for her nap and I went to Polly and Matt's. I suspected Matt would be at work but the children might be there. I let myself in through the cat flap and to my delight found Polly and Franceska in the kitchen.

'Alfie,' Franceska said, getting up to give me a stroke. 'I've seen so much of you this week.'

'I bet you want some lunch.' Polly smiled and got up. She opened a can of salmon and put it in a special bowl she kept just for me. She poured water into my water bowl too, which I was grateful for. Exercise left me thirsty. There was no sign of the children; I realized the boys were at nursery and school respectively and Martha was probably asleep. I curled up by the kitchen window and took a well-deserved rest as I listened to the chatter of the two women.

'The thing is, Aleksy doesn't talk to me,' Franceska said. 'I mean I ask him how is school and he just says "OK, Mama." But nothing else.'

'But you think something is wrong?' Polly looked concerned, as did I. I remembered the other day when he'd been a bit quiet, I thought he was about to tell me something when we were interrupted.

'He has some tears in his clothes, and he loses his things, like his pencil case. He seems quieter than normal and suddenly less keen on school.'

'Have you spoken to the school?'

'I've got an appointment with the head later, but you know you hear about bullying and how hard it is for children to talk about it. I can't bear it if someone hurts my Aleksy.'

'Of course you can't, Frankie, being a mum means we worry about them constantly. I get upset at playgroup when I see someone pushing one of mine, but the thought that we don't know what they are going through …'

'I know. Motherhood is wonderful but worry is the price.'

'And guilt.' Polly's eyes clouded over, briefly. 'Well, let me know what the school says and if there's anything we can do.

Aleksy and Matt are close, so maybe he can take him out for football and talk to him.'

'I would so very appreciate that.' Franceska's English was so much better than it had been when we first met but when she was upset, mistakes started to come through. 'His dad tries to talk to him but he's clammed up with him too.'

I felt a flutter in my chest. Things had been calm for so long that there was bound to be something else coming up. But Aleksy? I never expected that. I knew I would need to keep a close eye on this situation, as well as the new family. I had a feeling things were going to get busy again.

'What about the weekend? Why don't we meet up on Sunday?'

'Ah that would be great, we could all go to the park and maybe Matt could try to talk to Aleksy then. We've both tried but he won't …'

'Frankie, it's common for children not to want to worry their parents; they don't understand by not talking they worry us more. But we'll get to the bottom of it, I promise.' Polly reached over and grabbed Franceska's hands. I purred gently, happy to see another friendship that was so solid and knowing that I had been its foundation. It reminded me that I wanted to help people, both Aleksy and the new family. It was what I did.

I miaowed loudly and went to rub against Franceska's legs. Yes we would get to the bottom of it, I was determined. My to-do list was growing again.

-CHAPTER-
Eight

I fell asleep at some point after they left to pick up the boys and when I woke it was almost dark. I stretched out languidly; I had no idea how long I'd been asleep but it seemed like ages. I made my way back to Claire and Jonathan's. I was excited because Tasha, one of my other favourite humans was coming over for dinner with her partner Dave. Annoyingly, he was allergic to cats but when he came over he took some sort of pill to stop him sneezing. Everyone found it amusing but not me, I was affronted; it was no joking matter, having to take anti-cat pills. I used to say I would never trust a man who was allergic to cats but Dave seems OK and I love Tasha, so I have to accept him.

As I let myself back into the house, Claire was cooking and Jonathan was humming as he read the newspaper at the table. They both had drinks and they looked happy. As I sat by the door, head cocked to one side, watching them, I felt lucky yet again.

'Alfie,' they both said in unison as they greeted me. Jonathan and Claire smiled broadly at me. I nudged my bowl to tell them I was hungry.

'I'm on it, Alfie,' Jonathan said, going to the enormous fridge.

'Jonathan, he doesn't need to have smoked salmon. That's for breakfast tomorrow and I've got lots of cat food,' Claire stated, sounding cross.

I miaowed in protest.

'Hey, before I knew you existed, my darling, I gave him lots of fish. I can't stop that and just give him the rubbish you feed him.'

'He's spoilt.'

'He should be, he's an extraordinary cat.' Jonathan sliced the salmon and laid it in my bowl as if it was a five star restaurant. I licked my lips.

'He most definitely is.' Claire smiled indulgently.

By the time Tasha and Dave arrived, some very appealing smells were coming from the kitchen. I loved Tasha and when she visited, it reminded me of the days when it was just me and Claire and she was our first real friend. I rushed to greet them as Jonathan opened the door, getting gently scolded for getting in the way.

'Alfie, you're going to trip me up if you insist on getting under my feet,' he admonished as he opened the door. I was too eager, I know, but I was one excited cat.

'Hi,' Jonathan said, smiling and standing back to let Tasha and Dave in. Tasha immediately picked me up and Dave handed Jonathan some drinks and looked at me warily.

'Hi, Alfie,' he said, but I noticed he didn't get too close. I toyed with the idea of rubbing up against him to say hello, but realized that I just had to accept our arm's-length relationship and that I shouldn't be offended.

'Missed you, Alfie,' Tasha said as she carried me through to the kitchen. I revelled in her hug, she was so warm and caring, but there was something different about her tonight. I immediately sensed it. Something good, not bad, although I had no idea exactly what it was.

'Hi, Tash, oh you've got Alfie.' Claire leant in to kiss Tasha's cheek then Dave's who was close behind her.

'Right,' Jonathan said, 'drinks.' Tasha put me on the floor.

'Beer please, mate,' Dave asked.

'Tash?' Jonathan asked. 'We've got wine of every description.'

Tasha and Dave exchanged a look.

'Well, the thing is that I'm off alcohol,' she started.

'Why, what's wrong?' Claire asked. Her back was turned and she was emptying some posh crisps into a bowl.

'Well, actually nothing's wrong, it's just that I'm, well, we are pregnant!' Tasha laughed, happiness written all over her face. Dave beamed too, and Jonathan went and slapped him on his back.

'Great news, guys, congratulations.' He kissed Tasha's cheek. Claire froze for a moment, her face a picture of anxiety as she gripped onto the counter. I could see her struggle and then her fear. I willed her to say something; thankfully she turned around, plastering a smile to her face, composure resumed. My lovely Claire was instantly back.

'Wonderful news, Tash, Dave. Oh how brilliant.' She smiled, kissed and hugged her friends. I was able to exhale.

Over the evening, as there was chatter of babies between the women, I could sense Claire's underlying tension.

Although she was behaving naturally and they talked about all sorts of things, the evening had definitely become about Tasha.

'So do you think the acupuncture worked?' Claire asked.

'I don't know for sure, but it might have done. It certainly didn't do any harm.' Tasha smiled. 'I cannot believe how excited I am. I mean I know it's early days but, wow, it just all feels so amazing.'

'No sickness?'

'Oh yes, all day, not sure why they call it morning. But by evening I'm hungry, so thank you for doing dinner.' She laughed, her face was alive with joy.

'It's nothing special, if I'd known I might have produced something more suited to a special occasion,' Claire said.

'No shellfish or liver luckily,' Jonathan laughed.

'Oh get you,' Claire teased. 'Pregnancy expert.'

'Hopefully you guys won't be far behind us,' Dave offered. Claire concentrated on her food and didn't reply to that.

As the evening wore on, I noticed that Claire had drunk quite a lot; it was as if she had consumed Tasha's share of wine too. 'I'm so happy for you,' she kept saying over and over. I saw that Jonathan kept his arm protectively round his wife as they sat at the table and he didn't normally do that. Claire wasn't an alcoholic but when she was stressed she often drank quite a bit. She used to when she was unhappy and I didn't want her to go back to those days. But Tasha and Dave were so happy, radiantly, that they didn't seem to notice. They left shortly after polishing off their pudding, Tasha explaining that she was so tired she could barely keep her eyes open. As she kissed me goodbye I could only hope this baby didn't take after Dave in the cat allergy stakes.

When it was just the three of us once again, Jonathan cleared up while Claire nursed another drink. I set myself onto her lap, and she idly stroked me.

'Are you all right?' Jonathan asked, tension lining his face.

'I am, I mean I should be, but I'm worried, Jon. What if it doesn't happen for us?'

'OK, darling.' He put down the tea towel and sat beside her. 'Why are you thinking like this?'

'I should be happy when my best friend is pregnant but all I could think was that I wished it was me. That's not how I want to react.'

'Darling, we haven't been trying for as long as they have; it's only been a few months, so you can't start worrying about it.'

'Deep down I know that, but you know my history with anxiety. I'm not sure I can help it. I just worry about it all the time. I mean, everywhere I look, experts are all saying you should have your first baby in your early thirties and I'm not anymore.' She looked so upset I wanted to cry for her.

'OK, well why don't you go and see Tasha's acupuncturist; that can't hurt, and it's all natural. And you know anything you need to do to relax, we'll do, go for long walks, have massages, give up work if you want to.'

'Jonathan, I think that might be a bit extreme.' Claire laughed, sadly. 'And you hate walking.'

'I didn't exactly mean me. But I will do whatever it takes to make you happy. As long as you don't put my boxers in the freezer.'

'Why on earth would I do that?' Claire asked, echoing my thoughts.

'Pretend I didn't say that. I know, we'll go away for the weekend, somewhere romantic.' I narrowed my sleepy eyes. I instinctively knew that offer didn't include me. 'Claire, I know you want a baby but you can't let it get to you, not before we've even got a problem.'

'I know, Jon, I'll be OK, it's just I don't want to be the woman who is jealous of everyone else's baby news.'

'No, soon you'll be the woman *with* the baby news. I'm sure of it.' He stood up, took her hand, and kissed her. I jumped off her lap, as he led her to bed, and I went to my basket. I needed to curl up, think and sleep.

-CHAPTER-
Nine

I was up very early after being woken in the small hours by Jonathan who had to go to Germany for work. I didn't know where Germany was but I had gathered it was a different country. He had to go on a plane, which was a way that humans travelled, sort of on a giant bird that I had often watched flying overhead, and he would be gone for two days. He often went away for work and Claire said she liked it as she didn't have to pick up his dirty socks and she could read uninterrupted. I took this to mean she missed him terribly. I certainly did. I had two days of cat ready meals to look forward to.

Jonathan didn't even try to be quiet as he got ready to leave, banging doors, swearing as he stubbed his foot and waking me and Claire.

'Guten tag,' he said, while Claire groaned loudly. I followed him downstairs, trying to look my most charming, because I was hoping for my last nice breakfast. I was rewarded with tuna. I rubbed against Jonathan's legs to convey that I would miss him, and although he kept telling me to get off him in case I left fur on his smart trousers, I knew he appreciated it. I ate as he made coffee and munched a piece of toast before grabbing his overnight bag, and as Claire emerged from upstairs, he kissed her goodbye and was gone.

'He can be such a whirlwind, can't he?' Claire said, putting the kettle on and smiling warmly at me. I miaowed in agreement; Jonathan was like a ball of energy and that was one of the reasons we loved him, but the house was always calmer without him. We missed him but we also liked having a bit of peace and quiet, not that I would ever tell Jonathan that.

As Claire got ready for work I decided to go and see my new next door neighbours. I had hardly glimpsed Snowball or any of her family in the month that they'd been here. I'd taken to hanging out quite a bit by the loose fence panel but to no avail. My curiosity was reaching new heights and, not that I would admit it to anyone, I couldn't get Snowball's angelic face out of my head. I thought about her almost constantly, and I was in turmoil. I wanted so desperately to see her but I didn't know why, or even what I would do when I did. As I reached their back garden I crept forward to look into the house. I could see through the patio doors that the family were all at the kitchen table. The woman was wearing some kind of blue uniform, and she looked tired. The boy was slumped over a computer and was also wearing a uniform, but not like the mother. As I watched, the girl entered the room wearing an outfit similar to the boy but with a skirt rather than trousers. I gathered this was a school thing, like Aleksy only for older children. The man was making breakfast but sadly there was no sign of Snowball.

I was mesmerized, watching the scene from a well-placed bush. I wondered if I was a bit like a cat version of a stalker but then stalkers were bad and I had only good intentions. After a while the woman kissed everyone goodbye and made her way out of the room. Then the father passed two boxes to the children and looked as if he was hurrying them out. I couldn't make out what anyone was saying but suddenly the room was totally empty. I saw my chance.

It might not have been the most sensible thing ever, but before I knew it, certainly before I thought it through, I found myself at the other back door, creeping gently through the cat flap and into the house. As I stood in the kitchen, I wondered what to do next, but then I heard footsteps coming back towards the room. I quickly looked around and spotted an open cupboard. I leapt in it. The cupboard was full of cat food; pouches and boxes of biscuits, the sort Claire favoured.

'Come on, Snowball,' I heard the man say. 'I've laid your breakfast out.' I held my breath as I saw the man's legs. He walked towards the cupboard I was in so I quickly nestled behind a box, and before I knew what was happening, he pushed the door closed.

I blinked and adjusted to the darkness as I tried not to panic. I was trapped. I had no idea what would happen to me if the family found me in their cupboard and the thought made my heart beat loudly. I could almost hear it jumping out of my chest. I would be amazed if the cupboard wasn't shaking as much as I was. I crouched, trying to calm myself down, breathing slowly and trying to think positively.

'That's a good cat, Snowy, eat your breakfast,' the man said. I heard her purr, which sounded almost musical. 'Right then, I'm going to look for work again.' He paused. 'Not sure it's worth it, but I'm going to go upstairs and shut myself in my study, looking for jobs that don't exist and hoping something comes along to save us.' I heard his voice, laden with sadness, and wished I could see him, to see what was reflected on his face. 'Oh, Snowball, why do I feel that you're the only one who doesn't blame me?'

Snowball miaowed, gently. She was saying that she supported him.

'Well, talking to you, as lovely as it is, isn't going to get my family fixed. I'd better go.' After a few more moments I heard his footsteps moving away. I breathed again and thought about calling out. I was pretty sure Snowball would be able to open the cupboard, after all I could open them at home if I needed to. I weighed up the risks. On the one hand I would have to face Snowball's wrath, if she rescued me. On the other hand, I would have to stay in the cupboard and risk being discovered – and as she'd just been fed it could be hours. I decided to risk Snowball as it meant that at least I would get to see her. I miaowed as loudly as I dared.

'What on earth?' I heard her say, before I heard her paws padding outside the cupboard. I miaowed again. I could hear her scratching at the door and finally, after what seemed like an eternity, it opened a crack. She put her slender paw in and opened it fully. Finally we were face to face.

'Thank you,' I breathed, relief overtaking my fear.

'You again,' she hissed. Her beautiful eyes were full of anger.

'I'm sorry, Snowball. I'm Alfie, in case you'd forgotten. I just wanted to welcome you to the neighbourhood properly and … well … I …' I really hadn't thought this through.

'So you decided to break into my house and crawl into my food cupboard? What kind of maniac are you?' She looked so angry but so gorgeous at the same time. I almost swooned. I tried to muster all my charm.

'I just wanted to say hello, as I haven't seen you since you moved in. I'm just a friendly neighbour and want us to be friends.'

'I don't need friends, thank you very much,' she replied.

'We all need friends,' I replied. 'And from what I can tell, things aren't easy here.'

'That is none of your business,' she replied. This was one frosty cat.

'I just want to help. Why did you move here?'

'Alfie, I cannot decide if you are stupid or *very* stupid. I do not want you to be a friend. I do not want you here. Any problems my family have are our own and we don't need anyone else interfering.' She bared her teeth aggressively.

'I'm not trying to interfere, I just want to be supportive.'

'You are very stupid, I see. Now leave me in peace before I get really angry.' Her eyes flashed and she looked as if she might actually attack me. I knew I was beaten. For now.

'OK, I'll leave, but you know everyone needs friends, even you, and you know where I am when you need me.'

'Preferably never in my house again,' she hissed as I left.

I left her garden straight away and went to find Tiger. Snowball was all miaow and no bite I decided. She might not be welcoming me with open paws now, but I knew she would. I wasn't a cat to give up easily after all. It suddenly came to me. I would take her a house-warming gift, just like I did for Jonathan. A mouse. No, a bird. A bird was much more of a thoughtful gift, being harder to chase for us cats, and generally prettier. As I spotted Tiger outside her house I grinned. She was a better hunter, so I'd need to get her to help. Now I had a plan, it was only a matter of time before Snowball liked me; and with that wonderful thought, I left to put my plan into action, feeling as if I were floating on air.

-CHAPTER-
Ten

I left the bird for Snowball by her cat flap later that day. I waited for ages to give it to her in person, but there was no sign of her around and so I had no choice but to leave it. Tiger had helped me chase it, but I felt bad as I fibbed a bit and told her it was for one of my humans. You see, I was going to tell her who it was for but then when I told her I had been in the cupboard, and had a conversation with Snowball she had been really short with me. Especially when I mentioned again how beautiful I found her. If I didn't know better I would say that Tiger was jealous … but that made no sense. I tried to tell her that Snowball and her family needed help, but Tiger wouldn't listen to me. Instead she told me that, for once, perhaps I should stop being such an interfering cat and concentrate on those who actually cared about me. I didn't fully understand her hostility.

I was still pondering on the fact that two female cats in my life were less than pleased with me – although I knew I could get round Tiger easily enough – as I returned home. The house was empty although I knew that Claire was due back any minute. I gave myself a quick wash and waited for her by the front door. When I heard the key in the lock and the door open I miaowed. After the day I'd had, I needed someone to be nice to me.

'Hi, Alfie, it's not often you greet me at the door. Is it because you're worried I'm missing Jonathan?' She rubbed my neck which was one of my favourite things ever. I purred with delight.

After Claire showered and dressed, she fed me and poured herself a glass of wine. I ate quickly then we both sat together in the living room. Her with her book and me with my thoughts of Snowball. I was totally enchanted with her. The doorbell interrupted us and I rushed to see who it was.

'Polly,' Claire said, opening the door, 'come in quick, and have a glass of wine, we've just got time.'

I cocked my head to one side, puzzled. Time before what?

'Do you think we can sneak a bottle in? It might make it more bearable.'

'Pol, even a litre of Vodka wouldn't make this more bearable.' I wondered what they were talking about.

'I can't believe I have to go,' Polly moaned.

'Why do you?'

'We tossed a coin. Three times. I lost,' she replied.

'Yeah, well at least that's a bit fair. I'm convinced that Jonathan booked his business trip so he would miss the Neighbourhood Watch meeting.'

Ahh, I suddenly understood. It was the night of Heather and Vic's big gathering and no one looked forward to that. I decided I would go and see Matt, otherwise I'd be on my own all night and, as I was still a bit bruised from my day, I didn't fancy being alone.

'I guess you'll make him pay for that though,' Polly laughed.

'Don't you worry, if this is the hell I think it's going to be, then he will definitely pay.'

'Do you think your new neighbours will be there?' Polly asked.

'I don't know. You know what's weird is that I haven't seen them. I couldn't even tell you what they look like. I did go round a couple of times with a gift to introduce myself but there was no answer.' Like cat, like owner.

'I don't agree with the way Vic and Heather are behaving, acting as if the new family has something to hide but these guys aren't doing themselves any favours by keeping themselves to themselves,' Polly pointed out.

'I know, it's a bit strange. But then, I'm sure there's a perfectly reasonable explanation,' Claire replied.

'Let's hope so, for their sake, otherwise Vic and Heather will be rounding up a lynch mob before we know it.' They both laughed as they drained their wine and made their way out. I fleetingly wished I could have gone with them – I was intrigued to know what the meeting was actually going to be about, but of course with Salmon there I would be far from welcome. There was no way I was going to risk crossing his path.

I let myself into Matt and Polly's and found him sitting on the sofa, looking very pleased with himself.

'Ah, Alfie, nice of you to join me on my boys' night.' I saw he had a bottle of beer open on the coffee table. I miaowed and jumped on the sofa next to him. 'Ha, thank goodness I didn't have to go to that godawful meeting. You better make yourself comfortable; they're going to be gone hours.' He was smiling and I thought he was lucky Polly couldn't see him. She wouldn't be happy.

I smiled and curled myself up, nestling into him. As he put a film on the television I sighed contentedly. It was nice to relax at the end of a busy day.

'Matt,' I heard a voice shout. Startled, I opened my eyes, as did Matt. 'Wake up, boys, you were both snoring,' Polly stated.

'Sorry, I must have fallen asleep,' Matt said. I glared at Polly, blinking. I did not snore. Perish, the thought. 'What time is it?' he asked.

'Gone eleven. I'm so angry with you, and with you, Alfie, that neither of you had to endure the hell I did tonight.'

'So go on, what happened?' Matt looked as if he was trying hard not to smile, although he still looked as sleepy as I did.

'Well, where do I start? The new people didn't come, despite the fact that Heather and Vic had been knocking on their door daily and had also posted a number of flyers through their letter box. Apparently they did see the daughter of the family, a teenage girl who was on her way back from school, and she said that she was sorry but her parents were really up to their necks.'

'So of course they aren't going to accept that,' Matt said.

'They certainly are not. We tried to reason with Vic and Heather, reminding them that a month isn't long when you move house and perhaps they needed to give them a bit more time, but then of course they immediately jumped to conclusions, saying they obviously had something to hide. So after hours of speculation they no longer think the house is full of illegal immigrants, but it's a drugs den.' Polly shook her head.

'Based on what?'

'Nothing but the fact that they haven't shown themselves. Honestly, Matt, they're crazed! Apparently it's our duty, along with everyone else on the street, to watch the house – especially at night – and to report back.'

'You're kidding?'

'No, they even suggested drawing up a roster, but we all said that it wouldn't work. You know, we have lives. Jesus, Matt. And what's worse is that some of the other neighbours agreed with them – either they're mad too or they were too scared to argue. Anyway, they're having another meeting in a month, attendance is compulsory and you and Jonathan will have to go, my love.' It was Polly's turn to smile.

'Oh boy, that's something to look forward to. Drugs? Immigrants? This is going to be a barrel of laughs.'

As Polly and Matt hugged, and then started kissing like teenagers I saw it was time for me to take my leave. Matt and Polly had been together for years and years so I had no idea why they had to behave like that. I was going to alert them to the fact that I was going, but they looked so engrossed in each other that I quietly slunk out. I had a feeling I wouldn't be missed. As I entered my house and made my way upstairs I remembered again that Jonathan was away which meant that Claire would let me sleep on her bed. Yay! I punched my tail in the air in celebration. This day hadn't gone exactly to plan but it had ended well.

-CHAPTER-
Eleven

'Let me get this straight,' Tiger said. 'You're asking me to leave home at the crack of dawn and walk for miles to Aleksy's house?'

'Yes,' I replied, simply. Tiger and I were friends once again; her sulk had only been a short one.

I hadn't seen Snowball since the cupboard incident, over a week ago, and I knew better than to mention it to Tiger. I didn't even talk to her about the Goodwins' meeting, which I had also heard Claire discussing with Jonathan. She told him much the same as I'd heard from Polly, only adding that Vic and Heather said they would have their binoculars trained on the house at all times – meaning they might stray to our house. Jonathan had been pulling the blinds down just in case.

'Why, again?' Tiger pushed. I had explained it once but once was never enough for her. Tiger needed to hear everything at least twice before she seemed to understand it.

I had devised one of my plans. Franceska had been for lunch at Polly's. Strong, stoic Franceska, who was so much an anchor for all my families, was in tears as she explained that she had been to Aleksy's school but it seemed to have made no difference. The school explained that if Aleksy was, as Franceska and big Tomasz feared, being bullied, they had to either see it happening or Aleksy had to tell them, for them to take any action. But when asked, Aleksy kept saying he was fine. Despite the school saying that they would keep a close eye on things, Franceska wasn't convinced this was enough. Whilst Aleksy wouldn't tell them what was going on, he kept coming home covered in scratches and bruises – clear proof, Franceska said, that someone was hurting him.

My sweet Franceska was distraught. And my best human friend, Aleksy, had cried himself to sleep and Franceska didn't know what to do. It broke my heart, so I decided to take matters into my own paws. I would go to the school myself. I would find out what was wrong with Aleksy and I would fix it.

'Right, so I remember from my trip with Polly where they live. We have to leave very early because I don't know how long it'll take to walk, as I went in the pushchair last time. Anyway, when we get there we'll follow Aleksy to school.'

'Right, and then what?' Tiger looked at me as if I was mad. It was almost a fair assumption.

'Well, that's what I don't know.' I knew I had to get to Aleksy and show him that I was there for him. I also knew I had to sort out the bullying, if he was in fact being bullied, but I had no idea how exactly. What did people expect? I am a cat after all.

'So let me get this straight. We're going to walk miles but we don't even know what we're going to do when we get there? This might be one of your more genius ideas, Alfie. Maybe even better than the one involving nearly getting yourself killed by Joe, Claire's idiot ex-boyfriend.' I looked at Tiger; sarcasm was very unbecoming in a cat.

'All right, I know it's not perfect. But I cannot bear to think my Aleksy is sad. Tiger, I have to do something.' I was pleading.

'I know, I know.' She sounded exasperated. 'And after all you've been through there is no way I'm letting you go all that way on your own. No way. So I guess I have to come with you. But you owe me. Big time.'

'Oh thank you. I'll call for you tomorrow morning and I promise, I will make it up to you.' She looked at me, stretched out her paws and lifted her whiskers.

'I hope so, Alfie, I really do.'

'Tiger, you are the best friend any cat could have,' I said, as I bounded off home to rest up for the big journey.

It was still dark when I woke but the birds alerted me with the dawn chorus; it was my early morning alarm call and for once I was grateful for them, as I stretched and quietly padded downstairs and out of the cat flap. I went to Tiger's house and quietly made my way through her door, and found her drinking some milk. I was hungry but I knew I had no chance of breakfast before I left, so I would have to bear it. If I'd left any of my supper from the night before, Claire would have cleaned it away. Tiger's humans were a little less bothered with mess.

'Ready?' I whispered. She licked her whiskers and followed me outside. As I didn't venture far from home anymore, I felt nervous as we set off. I had paid very special attention to where we were going when I visited with Polly and luckily, the dark had no bearing on my senses. As we walked past Snowball's house, we both stopped and looked. Through the darkness a white flash chased a creature under a bush taking us by surprise.

'She's up early,' Tiger said looking at me. I glanced over at Snowball, who peered directly at us in her hostile way, but I didn't stop; I had bigger fish to fry. Oh how I wish I had a fish to fry in actual fact.

Snowball didn't move as we strode on. I thought it wouldn't hurt her to think I had lost interest; Jonathan always said women liked the chase, and he seemed to know a lot of women before settling down with Claire so maybe he was right.

'So you're not talking to Princess Mean then?' Tiger asked me as we headed towards the park.

'Tiger, today is about Aleksy, and you are with me, so let's leave the talk of Snowball.'

'Fine by me,' she replied.

The sky was slowly beginning to lighten as we walked; the air began to get warmer as the sun made its presence felt. Although I still felt a bit uneasy, as we got nearer to Aleksy's my confidence began to grow. The closer we got the more life appeared in the streets, as the world began to come alive. It was strange for me, being out at this time. Normally I would be fast asleep in my warm bed, but now, braving the biting dawn, I saw a different side of life and it made me realize how cosseted I had become.

Since my mission to find a new home after Margaret died, the long journey that led me to Edgar Road had put me off leaving there again. I rarely ventured further than the park at the end of the street. I looked over at Tiger, reassured by having her at my side.

'This is the street,' I said as we rounded a corner. I knew the flat would be easy to find as it was above the restaurant. So after walking a bit further, we arrived at our destination. The walk had taken a long time, but then we hadn't been rushing. Tiger wasn't one for running about after all. And we both made sure we took in every landmark so that we didn't have to worry about finding our way back again.

'This is it,' I said as we stood outside *Ognisko*. It was in darkness of course, and as we found a hiding place nearby I tried not to think about Franceska's sardines as my stomach rumbled.

'So what now?' Tiger asked.

'We wait for Aleksy to come out and follow him to school. But, it's important that they don't see us.'

'Why?'

'Because it'll be a surprise when I turn up.'

'And what are you going to do when you get there?'

'I don't know but I hope I'm going to get some inspiration.' To be honest, I didn't have a clue what I was dealing with and I had never, ever been in a school before. My plan wasn't without flaws.

'This better not be another dangerous situation you're getting us into again,' Tiger warned.

'They are children, not adults,' I pointed out. 'And anyway, once we get to the school I will be going in alone,' I said more bravely than I felt.

'I could come with you, find the bully, and scratch him really bad,' Tiger suggested, looking a bit too keen on the idea for my liking.

'No, Tiger, no violence. Not in this case. The bully might be nasty, and goodness knows if he is, I dislike him for hurting Aleksy, but he's still a child.'

'OK. If you insist, I'll just watch you and not interfere.' Tiger bristled. She seemed almost disappointed that she wasn't going to get to inflict pain on someone.

'Thank you,' I replied and we waited in silence.

After what felt like a long time, I saw little Tomasz first as he appeared out of the front door, jumping, full of energy. Franceska was next and she turned and spoke, before Aleksy appeared. He was looking sad and I could sense his reluctance in the way he looked and moved. Tiger and I hung back and then began to follow them in silence. It was easy to keep out of sight, by dodging behind the odd fence or bush. Whereas Tomasz chatted animatedly to his mother, Aleksy was largely silent as he dragged his feet.

'Oh look, there's the school,' Tiger said and we stopped and hid by a parked car. We watched as Franceska and the boys crossed the road.

'I'm glad it wasn't too far,' I said as I looked. 'So that's their school.' I was quite excited to see where Aleksy and little Tomasz spent their days. I had seen schools before, of course, in passing but I had never been in one before.

There were children everywhere. As Franceska dropped the boys at the gate they went through it and into the playground, a noisy tarmacked area, swarming with loud little people. Tomasz ran off in one direction and Aleksy stayed close to the gate. As Franceska turned, shooting a last worried look at Aleksy before walking off, that was my cue.

'OK,' I said as Tiger and I crossed the road. 'Stay by the gate. If anything bad happens I'll make my loudest noise.'

'Good luck, Alfie,' Tiger said, nuzzling my neck. I felt tense again as I squeezed through the bars of the gate and into the playground. I followed Aleksy as he made his way across the playground to a big building. Then I saw a group of children. One of them waved at Aleksy, but another child, a little bigger than Aleksy, stopped him.

'Here's the cry baby,' he said nastily. I looked at all the boys and girls. None of them looked comfortable with the horrible boy but I could see that they were all too scared to say anything.

'Leave me alone,' Aleksy said, although I could hear the wobble in his voice.

'Make me.' All the other children looked aghast at the two boys. No one seemed to know what to do.

'I don't want to fight with you,' Aleksy said. I wanted to fight him though. I wanted to give this kid a good hard swipe – but I told myself violence wasn't the answer.

'Because you are a baby and a chicken.' The boy started to make chicken noises as he came very close to Aleksy. 'I guess I'll just take your lunch,' he said.

'No … you can't have it,' Aleksy stammered back. I was proud of him; I could see he was scared, but he was still sticking up for himself.

'I think you'll find I can.'

I wondered where the adults were. I spotted one but she was the other side of the playground and hadn't noticed what was going on.

I realized that children weren't so different from adults. You got nice ones and mean ones, but as I watched, I saw that this was just a sad kid who was acting tougher than he actually was. I couldn't tell Aleksy this though, so I decided that it was time for me to act.

I moved towards Aleksy and miaowed loudly.

'Alfie,' he said, startled, fear forgotten. 'What are you doing here?' He picked me up. I purred into him.

'Is that your cat?' one of the children asked.

'Yes, well he lives in my old road, not at my house, but he's very clever. He must have followed me all the way to school!' Aleksy put me down and all the children rushed to pet me. I made myself my most charming as I purred and revelled in the attention.

'It's only a stupid cat,' the nasty boy said. I wasn't scared though, he didn't really pose as much of a threat as many adults and other animals I'd met. After all, I'd once had a seagull threaten me and a horrid man nearly kill me. This was nothing compared to that. But I was powerless as the nasty boy took Aleksy by surprise and grabbed the bag off his back. Aleksy grappled with him but there was nothing I could do as the bag swung out and hit a little girl in the face. I seemed to be the only one who noticed as the girl burst into tears and ran off; both boys scrambled to grab the bag. Aleksy won. I looked over at the crying little girl, torn about what to do – I was here to protect Aleksy, but I knew I could quickly cheer her up if I went over and snuggled up to her.

But before I could decide, the bully looked at Aleksy who was now clutching the bag to his chest, then at me. As if weighing up his next move he stepped towards me. I stood my ground, looked at him and hissed aggressively. The boy looked a bit startled and quickly stumbled back.

'See, he doesn't like you. He only likes nice people,' Aleksy said, looking and sounding a bit braver. The other children laughed too.

The boy looked at Aleksy, his eyes full of anger, and then he looked at me.

'Dumb cat,' he said. I flicked my tail up in anger, and hissed at him again. He backed away.

'Ha, Ralph is afraid of a cat,' Aleksy said. I realized then, as Aleksy's eyes sparkled that although I hadn't done much, I had given Aleksy confidence – and that was exactly what he needed. As all the other children laughed, a bell rang out. I stuck close to Aleksy; I wanted to see more of this school, it seemed an intense but interesting place.

It was both scary and exciting as I seemed to be caught up in a sea of legs, making their way into what I learned was a classroom. There were a lot of children, all chattering loudly as I stayed close to Aleksy. I managed to follow him into the room, sneaking past a lady they called 'Miss Walton'.

Ralph was red faced and clearly not happy. As the children competed to sit near Aleksy he had the biggest smile on his face. Meanwhile, Ralph sat on his own.

'Right, time for the register,' Miss Walton said, not having spotted me yet. She looked quite young and smiled a lot. As one by one the children answered to their names I began to enjoy myself.

'Molly?' Miss Walton said. There was silence. 'Has anyone seen Molly?' she asked, looking concerned.

'She was in the playground, Miss,' one child pointed out; I guessed they meant the little girl who had been hit by Aleksy's bag. I felt terrible for having forgotten her, and knew that I had to help them find her.

I miaowed very loudly. The teacher looked over and saw me jump onto Aleksy's desk, making everyone laugh.

'Hi, and who are you?' she asked, as she came over.

'This is Alfie, he lives in my old street but he is a very special cat,' Aleksy said proudly. 'He must have followed me to school today and it's very far.'

'Well hello, Alfie,' she said, stroking me. 'But you're not allowed to be in school, I'm afraid. This is for humans only.' She laughed and I miaowed again. I jumped off the desk and, yowling as loudly as I could, started to walk towards the door.

'Oh please can he stay?' Aleksy asked. The others all cried out in agreement. All apart from Ralph who looked at his feet.

'No, I'm afraid not. Look, children, all stay here and I'll take Alfie out and find Molly.' Another adult came into the classroom; Miss Walton said something to her about being back in a minute and then as I ran out she started to follow me. I tried to remember the way I'd come in as I legged it towards the exit. Before I left, I needed to find Molly, I'd seen her run off after all and had an idea which way she'd gone.

'Alfie, slow down,' Miss Walton said as she hurried after me. I stood in the playground, finding my bearings and sniffing the air. Like a super sleuth, I made my way round the side of the building where I had seen Molly heading following my nose, vaguely aware of Miss Walton a little way behind me. I stopped in front of a shed, noticing a door was ajar, just big enough for a small child – or a cat – to slide through. I peered in, but it was dark and cramped, full of outdoor clothes – muddy wet weather wear and Wellington boots. From the door, I couldn't see the girl but I could sense her. Miss Walton came up behind me a little breathless.

'Molly,' she called. 'Molly, are you in there?' Her words were met with silence and I looked up and saw the worry etched on Miss Walton's face as she looked around her, panic growing. I miaowed and went inside, scrambling around in the darkness, getting caught up in raincoats, and tangled in boots but determined to find Molly.

She was hiding in a dark corner, curled up and still crying. I miaowed loudly again, running out to alert the teacher. She looked puzzled – she was running around the playground shouting Molly's name and sounding increasingly frantic. I kept yelling at her, brushing her legs before running back to the shed. She looked uncertain as she followed me into the shed but I led her to the missing girl.

'Molly, there you are,' Miss Walton said, kindly, her eyes full of concern and voice full of relief. I quite liked this teacher; she was very warm. Molly looked up, her eyes teary and I saw her nose was bleeding. 'Oh, Molly, what happened?'

'I got hit by a bag. Ralph was trying to fight Aleksy, and it hit me.' She burst into tears again.

'Come on, we'll get you cleaned up.' Miss Walton pulled Molly up and, holding her hand, went back inside. Of course I followed them, even though I knew I shouldn't, but I needed to see how this story ended.

Miss Walton took Molly to another kind lady who said she would make her better and then she headed back to the classroom. I managed to sneak in behind her.

'Oh, Alfie,' she said as she noticed me again. 'I forgot about you.'

'Alfie!' Aleksy cried. 'I thought you were sending him home.'

'I was, but, Aleksy, you were right, Alfie is a very special cat. He found Molly, and he's the hero of the school today.' All the children cheered me and I preened myself. It hadn't been hard but then again, I wasn't going to refuse praise. Milking it, I first went up to where Aleksy sat and jumped onto his desk. As the rest of the class crowded round him I stood on my back legs and raised my paw. 'However, I have heard that there was an altercation in the playground which we will talk about, mark my words.' Miss Walton looked at Ralph who turned red and looked as if he would burst into tears.

'High-five,' Aleksy said, as I sat up, tapping my paw with his hand. A trick we practised every time I saw him. I was quite an old paw at it now, in fact.

'Wow, can I do that?' another child asked. I let them all high-five me, which was tiring but it made them so happy that I couldn't refuse. Even Ralph was moving closer, but he didn't seem quite able to join in.

'Aleksy, you know the coolest cat ever. Can I come and see him at your house, if he's ever there?' one child asked. As everyone made a request to hang out with Aleksy and me, I felt as if my job here was done.

'But Alfie really does have to go now,' Miss Watson said all too soon, 'so how about we write a story about him, and his journey here? Then we can all draw pictures!'

'Yeah,' the class chorused, excitedly.

'Great,' she said. 'Right, while I show Alfie out, yet again, you can all start thinking about the story.' She picked me up and took me outside. When we got to the gate she put me down. 'Bye, Alfie, nice to meet you but it's best if you don't make this a regular thing,' was her parting comment.

'All OK?' Tiger said, as she came to greet me.

'Mission accomplished I think, and it was incredibly easy! Aleksy is very popular now and that horrible boy isn't going to bother him again.' Seeing how the children had reacted to Aleksy, I was confident of that. I wished I could have been there to hear their story about me though. I would have liked that.

CHAPTER
Twelve

'All right, I said I'd go,' Jonathan said reluctantly, as I appeared in the kitchen. It was the day after my school adventure and he had arrived back from his work trip.

'Take the plant I bought them before it dies,' Claire snapped. She had bought it about a week after Snowball's family moved into number 48, and as all attempts she'd made to deliver it had been in vain, she'd been watering it herself.

I bristled, she clearly wasn't in the best of moods.

'Of course, darling. Hey, are you all right?' His voice was tender so I knew he was as concerned as I was.

'Yes, sorry I snapped. I just think those poor neighbours need warning about the horrors opposite them. I saw Vic today and he's really got it in for them.'

'OK, I'll give it a go, wish me luck.' He kissed his wife. 'Alfie, come with me, you haven't met the new neighbours yet either have you?'

How little he knew. However, unable to resist another glimpse of Snowball, I trotted off.

I wondered if Vic and Heather were watching as Jonathan stood on the doorstep and rang the bell. I was sure I could see a curtain twitch. Jonathan was quite insistent with the bell, and after what seemed like ages we heard footsteps coming towards us. It was the man who opened the door. Although he only opened it a fraction.

'Hello?' he said, suspiciously. What was it with these people?

'Hi, I'm Jonathan, your next door neighbour. We wanted

to welcome you to Edgar Road.' The man opened the door a bit more.

'Hi, I'm Tim. Sorry we haven't introduced ourselves but it's been pretty hectic.' Tim sounded normal, not the way he had when I had heard him speaking to Snowball where his voice had been sad. Suddenly she appeared at his feet as the men shook hands.

'Nice to meet you, Tim. Oh and this is my cat, Alfie.'

'Snowball,' he said, gesturing to her. Both men laughed awkwardly. Snowball looked at me through narrowed eyes; she clearly wasn't over the moon to see me.

'My wife, Claire, got a plant for you.' Jonathan handed it over, looking a bit sheepish. It wasn't very manly after all. 'She's been over but you must have been out.'

'To be honest, we're not home much. My wife, Karen, works shifts at the hospital and poor thing is doing killer hours at the moment. The kids have just started a new school, which, well, you know how it is.'

'We don't have children, yet.' I marvelled at the fact Jonathan disclosed this information, he looked a bit bashful so I guessed he was surprised by his openness too.

'Well take it from me, teenagers starting a new school is no fun,' he laughed although it was edged with bitterness.

'Sorry to hear that. Anyway, listen, we should grab a beer? Or maybe you and your wife would like to come over for dinner one night?'

'We'd love to but to be honest at the moment things aren't easy. Karen's working all hours and with the kids …'

'Well, when you have time the invitation's there. Anyway, I wanted to warn you that there's this couple over the road, Vic and Heather Goodwin. They're Neighbourhood Watch

Nazis, and they've got a bit of a bee in their bonnet.' Jonathan scratched his head, awkwardly. Snowball stared at me, with beautiful but frosty eyes. I had to make myself concentrate on the conversation, she was so distracting.

'Really?'

'They are sort of, well, curtain-twitchers my mate Matt calls them. They think that as they haven't met you and you didn't come to the meeting the other night, you're, well, you know … dodgy.' Jonathan looked a bit red, and Snowball scowled at me. Tim bristled.

'Dodgy, because we didn't go to a meeting? Christ what kind of place is this?'

'Oh, no don't get the wrong idea! It's just them, and I'm warning you because, well, they kind of have their binoculars trained on your house.' He laughed again.

'My God, you are kidding me.' Tim looked across the street. I turned and could swear the curtains did in fact twitch again. 'This is crazy. Look, we just like to keep ourselves to ourselves, so thanks for the plant but, really, I have to go.'

'Please, I didn't mean to offend you, it was just a friendly visit.' Poor Jonathan looked confused.

'Bye, Jonathan.' Before he could say anything else, Tim closed the door.

'Damn Alfie, I think I messed up.' Jonathan looked flummoxed. 'Claire's going to kill me,' he mumbled as he walked away. I stayed put, trying to figure out what went wrong.

All of a sudden I heard raised voices, but Jonathan was already out of earshot.

'I hate school, this house and this stupid place, why can't we just go home,' a female voice shouted – the teenage girl I thought.

'Because, Daisy, you know full well what happened. We have no choice.' It was Tim and he sounded desperate.

'Yeah well that doesn't make it any better does it,' a surly boy's voice chipped in.

'For the love of God, I can't do anything right and now we've got the neighbours on our backs,' Tim shouted.

'Can we all calm down,' a voice obviously belonging to Karen said. 'It's not your dad's fault and if we continue like this our family is going to fall apart.' Her voice was desperate. Then I heard noisy tears, which I thought was the girl again. My head was so close to the door, I was almost in it.

'Alfie!' Snowball's voice came from behind the door, I pricked up my ears.

'Yes?' I hoped my voice conveyed helpfulness.

'Go away and leave us in peace. None of us, especially not me, need you here.' Her voice was even more vehement than usual.

'I was only trying to help,' I said.

'You can help by leaving us alone, all of you. Oh and by the way, if it was you that left me the bird the other day, you shouldn't have bothered.' I heard her padding away, as the other voices faded and I had no alternative but to turn around and head home.

Whatever was going on with them, it wasn't good, although I knew, instinctively, that they weren't bad people or doing anything dodgy like the Goodwins thought. But I could tell they also needed help, although, boy, they weren't making it easy, that was for sure.

I made my way back and saw Jonathan standing, still looking confused, key in hand. I was about to run after him to follow him in when a shadow blocked my path. It was Salmon.

'Oh, not you,' I hissed.

'Alfie, you really are a silly cat. Those people are bad and that white ball of fluff is no better. She's an evil cat.'

'How on earth would you know?'

'My owners know, and if you know what's good for you you'll steer clear. They are going to be very fleeting visitors on Edgar Road, my family will see to that.'

'What do you mean?' I suddenly felt very fearful.

'They rent that house and the landlord won't put up with illegal activity.'

'What illegal activity?' My eyes widened.

'We don't know yet but rest assured we will get to the bottom of it.'

'So it's just what you guys think?' I almost laughed.

'Don't take us seriously if you don't want to, but mark my words, we will see this street returned to the way it should be.'

'Salmon, you're mad. You have no idea what you're talking about.' Salmon went to swipe me with his paw but I was too quick as I dodged out of his way. 'I'm not going to fight you. I just think you've got it wrong.'

'Do you now? Well just wait, and then we'll see who is the mad cat around here.' Salmon gave me another glare as he flicked his tail and moved aside to let me pass.

CHAPTER

Thirteen

After the drama of the previous day I was happy to welcome my favourite day. Once a month, on a Sunday, all my families came together. They all brought food and the children played together. It was so much fun for me to see them all under one roof – all the people I loved. So I put my thoughts of Snowball and my altercation with Salmon aside to revel in what was important to me; love.

Although that brought me back to Snowball. I was feeling towards her the way that I think some human men and women feel about each other. I was pretty sure that I was falling for her romantically. The way I felt when I saw her was almost electric. I felt a current running through my veins and my fur almost stood on end. And when I didn't see her, I was consumed by thoughts of her. I had taken to pining by the loose fence panel a bit too often, desperate to catch even just a glimpse of her. I had it bad.

When the doorbell went my fur was almost shivering with excitement as I stood ready to welcome everyone. Aleksy and Tomasz bounded in and rushed up to me, then Franceska, and Tomasz followed, carrying bags and handing over food and wine as they greeted Jonathan and Claire. I enjoyed being fussed by all of them, especially Aleksy who I was gratified to see was like his old self, with a big smile on his face and the sparkle back in his eyes. I rolled over, purred and snuggled as I enjoyed welcoming my guests in the best way ever.

Before we could catch our breath, the doorbell went again heralding Polly, who was holding Henry's hand, and Matt who was carrying Martha. The excitement of the children was fever-ish as I yet again enjoyed being cuddled and stroked. When the initial excitement died down, everyone went into the kitchen. As Tomasz and Claire sorted out the food, the back doors were opened and the children, except for Martha, headed out.

Although Jonathan's garden was small, there was a lawn and Aleksy had brought his football so they started chasing it around. I was about to join them, but Franceska picked me up.

'You will not believe what happened,' she said.

'What?' Jonathan asked, he had a big smile on his face as he watched the boys playing.

'Alfie went to Aleksy's school.' The room was silent as everyone looked at me.

'How on earth did he manage that?' Matt asked, scratching his head.

'We don't know, but we think he must have found his way to our flat and followed us there.'

'Good grief, Alfie, sometimes I wish you could talk because I would love to know how you do these things,' Claire said, looking amazed. I miaowed and they laughed.

'So,' Tomasz continued. 'You know how Aleksy was having problems with a boy at school.'

'He was being bullied, Tomasz. He was very bad,' Franceska added.

'Yes, well we went to the school but without knowing the full story there was not much they could do,' big Tomasz said.

'Aleksy wouldn't tell us what was going on,' Franceska added.

'What's this got to do with Alfie?' Polly asked. I miaowed again.

'Well he went to Aleksy's school, followed him to class and everyone in the class was really excited; so now he is popular and they are doing a school project with a story and drawings about Alfie! The boy leaves him alone now and tries to be his friend.'

'You're telling me that Alfie went to the school and sorted out a bully?' Jonathan looked at me in disbelief.

'Yes, he did. He really did!' Franceska was excited.

'So they're doing a project on him?' Matt asked, looking perplexed.

'Yes, they have written a story as a class and everyone, even the bad boy, has made a painting of him.'

I felt so emotional as I listened to Franceska explain. My plan had worked and, admittedly, I was trying very hard not to feel too smug about it. I was enjoying the praise and I was also enjoying the fact that my humans were so confused about my actions; I liked to keep them on their toes.

'It'd be nice for him to go and see the paintings,' Claire suggested, echoing my thoughts.

'Why don't we take him?' Franceska suggested. 'I could take him! Would you like that, Alfie?' I purred in the affirmative.

'Alfie, I do love you but you certainly do my head in at times,' Jonathan said, which I knew was a compliment, as I jumped out of Franceska's arms and headed outside to play football, or paw-ball more accurately.

As Polly, Franceska and Claire cleared up after lunch, the men put on a film for the children. I padded between both rooms, keeping an eye on everyone. Martha was asleep on the sofa while the boys – adults included – watched the film. The doorbell interrupted us and Jonathan reluctantly tore himself away to answer it. Vic was on the doorstep, without Heather for once.

'We have company,' Jonathan said, gruffly before the man had a chance to speak.

'I won't stop but I need to call an emergency meeting. Tomorrow night at our house.'

'What on earth for?' Jonathan asked.

'Your next door neighbours. I have Heather on watch right now.' Jonathan looked around Vic and saw Heather behind her living room curtains with her binoculars.

'She's hardly inconspicuous,' Jonathan said.

'Well,' Vic replied. 'The time for that has gone. Something has happened and I can tell you it is very serious.'

'What?' Jonathan asked.

'The police have been round. I'm surprised you missed it. They stayed for ages which goes to show that we're right to be concerned. I am calling their landlords in the morning and I'll see you tomorrow evening, seven sharp so we can discuss what we're going to do.' Before Jonathan could reply again, Vic turned and walked off, leaving him standing dumbfounded on the doorstep.

As Jonathan explained the visit to the others, I wondered what on earth the police were doing at Snowball's house. I was sure that there was nothing bad about Snowball and her family, but it seemed as though there was no convincing the Goodwins.

'The thing is that he was a bit odd when I went around,' Jonathan said. 'I hate to think Vic is right about anything, but I just don't know.'

'And we did send round a plant, and not a word,' Claire replied. 'I mean if it was me I would drop round to say thank you at least.'

'They do seem to be a bit strange. I saw the kids the other day, well teenagers really,' Polly continued. 'But I haven't caught a glimpse of the parents.'

'Although it does sound as if the Goodwins are on a bit of a witch hunt,' big Tomasz pointed out.

'You know what they're like. Anyway, the upshot is that whether that family are drug barons, gangsters or even just perfectly normal people, they're making our lives a misery because we have to go to another meeting. I almost want to evict them on that basis,' Jonathan mused.

'Just don't go,' Franceska suggested. I loved how sensible she was but also so naive. She escaped the Goodwins when she lived here, so she had no idea how awful they were.

'We can't not go, it's not an option,' Matt said.

'Luckily, boys, it's your turn to go, so Jonathan and Matt, all I can say is have fun,' Polly laughed.

'And I won't wait up,' Claire finished with a wink.

-CHAPTER-
Fourteen

'I have to warn her,' I said to Tiger.

'Oh, Alfie, if only you paid half as much attention to your real friends, rather than to someone who doesn't seem to have a nice word for you.'

'I know, but you know as well as I do what unhappiness can do. Look at how I fixed things for Aleksy. I need to do the same for Snowball, or at least try to. I'm pretty sure her family's unhappiness is the reason she is so prickly after all. So if I can help her family, I can help her.'

I tried to snuggle up to Tiger, but she moved away from me. She wasn't a happy kitty. She had wanted us to go and play with the other cats but I couldn't. After all, my neighbours were in trouble with the Goodwins and I wanted to give Snowball the chance to do something about it.

'Look, Tiger, I'll go over there, and try to get her attention then I'll come and join the rest of you. I'm sorry but you know what I'm like and a cat's got to do what a cat's got to do.' I gave her my most endearing look as she stalked off. But she looked back at me and I knew that she would forgive me, yet again. Eventually.

After Tiger stalked off I made my way to Snowball's back garden. I didn't exactly have a plan, but I was hoping that it would come to me when I got there. Although of course I was determined not to be so stupid as to get stuck in any cupboards today. The weather was damp and threatened rain. I felt this in my back legs especially. It was funny but my injury seemed to be affected by the weather. I felt a dull ache in my leg as I prepared to gently jump over the back fence and into Snowball's garden.

I let my thoughts wander to earlier this morning. We had been up early and as I bounded downstairs eager for breakfast, I saw something on our doormat. I miaowed to draw Claire's attention to it. It was a white envelope with their names written on it. Claire opened it and pulled out a card. Later when Jonathan came down, ready for work she showed him.

'So they sent a thank you for the plant after all,' he said, giving the note a quick glance.

'Yes but, darling, it just says, "Thank you for the plant it was a very kind thought, from Tim, Karen, Daisy and Christopher." Not much really.'

'At least they have manners. Strange they didn't ring the doorbell to say hello when they dropped it off though. We went to bed quite late last night, and you were up early so they must have put it through the letterbox either incredibly late or very early.'

'Which is weird, Jonathan. I hate to give any credence to the Goodwins but it is strange.'

'Maybe,' Jonathan said, taking a sip of coffee and buttering a piece of toast, 'they seem to be nocturnal. Like bats. Like Batman.' His eyes were wide.

'You're saying Batman lives next door?' Claire raised her eyebrows exasperated.

'A whole bat family. By day they're mild-mannered, by night they turn into bats and clean up the evil streets around Edgar Road.'

'You're as insane as the Goodwins.'

'But it is a good theory for me to bring up at the meeting

tonight. That will throw them off,' he chuckled.

'Almost makes me want to come along.' Claire kissed the top of his head.

'You still can you know,' he replied.

'I said almost.'

As I jumped down onto their lawn, I stopped short; the girl, who I now believed was called Daisy, stood in the garden smoking a cigarette and looking at her mobile phone. I stood still, unsure what my next move should be, when she turned and screamed.

'God, you startled me,' she said, but didn't sound angry. She bent down and looked at my tag. 'Hello, Alfie. You are a very pretty cat.' I tilted my head to one side and blinked in greeting. I would have preferred being called handsome but I would take pretty. I purred as she put out the cigarette and stroked me. Then she sat down on the back step, looking pensive. This was my chance, I thought as I rubbed up against her legs. She was wearing school uniform and as it was late morning I wondered why she wasn't at school. I glanced through the patio doors, but the house looked deserted.

'Oh boy,' she said stroking me. 'I wish I knew what to do.' I nestled into her, knowing that she needed to talk and I needed to listen. 'I'm bunking off school, which I've never done before. But then I was forced to leave my old school when we moved here and I'm in the middle of my exams! I mean I know what happened meant we *had* to move but that doesn't make it any easier.' She let out a huge sigh.

I miaowed softly, urging her to go on as she wasn't exactly making anything clear to me.

'I know I shouldn't blame Dad, but Chris is miserable, Mum's working herself into the ground, and it wasn't his fault but still … we're all suffering. How can life change so drastically, so quickly? I'll never understand that.'

I miaowed again, I totally understood that one. After all, I'd been there. My situation had brought me to Edgar Road, and I hadn't wanted life to change when it did either.

'I wish I could feel better about it. I just feel so angry about everything all the time.' She pulled gently at my fur in the nicest way. Lucky Snowball I thought. 'And so does everyone. This is one unhappy house, that's for sure.'

She stood up.

'Anyway, Alfie, I'd better go to school before they call my parents and there's even more shouting here.' She started walking away, then turned around. 'Have you met my Snowball?' she asked.

I miaowed. She laughed.

'She'd like you. I think you'd make a really cute cat couple.' She laughed sadly and I felt my stomach flutter. If only, I thought.

I stared at the empty house, contemplating whether or not to go in given that the house was empty – I was a curious cat after all – when I heard a hiss behind me. Although it was aggressive, it was still music to my ears. I turned around.

'Hi,' I said.

'When are you going to get the message and leave us alone?'

'Where were you when I was talking to Daisy?'

'You spoke to Daisy?' Snowball looked angrier than ever as she bared her teeth.

'She told me a bit about how she was forced to move here.' I really hoped she would soften towards me as I gave her my best smile.

'Yes we had to move and because of Karen's work we ended up here. Everyone is living on a knife-edge and now the police are involved. The kids had to leave their very nice school and no one is happy about it. Including me.' She looked horrified.

'So why do you all keep to yourselves?' I asked, my eyes like saucers as I felt desperate to know more.

'Oh goodness, I have said too much. Forget I said anything and please, you need to leave us alone. We've had enough of people interfering in our life, causing trouble, we are better off alone. My family are good people but they have been through hell, through no fault of their own.' She paused, then thankfully spoke again. 'Tim has been the victim of injustice, and the rest of the family are suffering. We had to leave our old home and we need to be left alone.'

'Snowball, I do understand that you might feel that way. Life hasn't been all sardines and butterflies for me you know.'

'What's that got to do with us?' Snowball asked.

'I just want you to know I've been in a similar position. You don't know my story but before I lived here I was left orphaned and they were going to put me in a shelter. I became a homeless cat and I nearly died making my way here. When I got here I finally found homes but it was awful before that, so you see I do know how hard life can be.' I was desperate for her to see that I did care but it wasn't exactly going to plan. 'But, Snowball, I'm only trying to help. I can help you, I just know I can, I can make your family happier, by introducing them to my families. But you have to give me a chance. Daisy talked to me, why can't you?'

'I don't think so,' she said, quietly.

'But you know we need to do something. People are talking behind your backs, the Goodwins are relentless, if only you'd let me help, I could solve this for you.'

'It's not something you, I or anyone can solve.' She quickly switched back to being hostile just as I felt that we were getting somewhere as she flicked her tail at me, turned on her paws and had her back to me.

'What happened to you all?' I asked, softly.

'I've said too much. Please go, give us some space. We'll figure it out.' Without even a backward glance she jumped through the cat flap and was gone.

Although I was left with more questions than answers, I had made some progress. I would do exactly what I said to Snowball and I would bring our families, and therefore us, together.

I lay on my back on a sunny patch of grass in Polly and Matt's front garden, watching the sky and thinking. There was no sign of anyone at home but that was OK. I did quite fancy something to eat but it was more important to me to ponder on what had been happening and what I could do about it.

As Snowball's face popped into my head I felt giddy. Yes, she was angry but that didn't stop her beauty shining through. I couldn't stop thinking about her glittering eyes and that incredible white fur … I had never felt this way about another cat before, and I wasn't sure exactly how to describe it, but all I wanted was to be close to her.

A loud miaow jolted me out of my reverie and I rolled back onto all fours. My friend Rocky stood in front of me.

'How long have you been there?' I asked, stretching out; my back legs felt stiff and I realized I must have been sunbathing a bit longer than I thought.

'Only a few minutes. You looked so content, with the biggest smile on your face.'

'I was thinking of Snowball,' I admitted. 'You know, the white cat who's just moved in down the street.'

'I know who you mean. I bumped into her a few evenings ago, although she was pretty rude to me. I thought for a minute she was going to attack but she was just warning me not to try to talk to her.'

'She can be aloof,' I said, knowing I was trying to make excuses for her.

'I think that might be your best understatement yet, Alfie. Besides, Tiger was just telling us all about her.'

'What was Tiger saying?' I narrowed my eyes.

'That she's nasty but you seem intent on sucking up to her. She's not best pleased with your behaviour, and she's guessed that you have a crush on her.'

'Is that what this is? Tiger's not wrong though. I can't stop thinking about that fluffy white coat, and those eyes …'

'Oh boy, you've got it bad, Alfie. Let me give you some advice, man to man; be careful, women are complicated. Take Tiger for example.'

'Tiger? I barely think of her as a female cat.'

'That's the problem, Alfie, you two are such good friends but she is female and, well, it's kind of difficult to be really close friends with girls. If you know what I mean.'

'I absolutely don't.' I really didn't get it. I was friends with Agnes, the cat from my first home, I was friends with the human women in my life, so why not Tiger?

'OK, well Tiger has this little thing for you, you know, more than just friends. She has, you know, romantic feelings for you.'

I nearly fell off my legs. I couldn't believe what I was hearing.

'There must be some mistake, Rocky, she doesn't think of me like that.'

'Well, mate, trust me she does, you just don't notice. You should have heard her just now. She's really jealous.'

'Jealous?!' This was all news to me.

'Oh, Alfie, you silly cat. You need to be careful if you don't want to lose Tiger as your friend.' Rocky sat down, looking serious. 'She won't ruin your friendship but you need to respect her feelings, especially if you really do like Snowball.'

'You've given me even more to think about; thank you for being a good friend. I really do care about Tiger, she is my best cat friend and I don't want to hurt her. But I can't stop thinking about Snowball.' Rocky and I looked at each other, seriously.

'Hey, Alfie, that's what friends are for. I'd better go – lunch is calling.'

We said goodbye and I suddenly felt I had the weight of the world on my shoulders. How much could my head take? Now I had even more to figure out and solve. I felt as if I might explode.

I made my way back to my house. My cat instinct told me it would be safer to keep out of the way of anyone for now, as I made my way round the back and in through the cat flap. The house would be empty, I could find some peace and quiet and try to get things straight.

As I stalked through the kitchen and was about to go and find my favourite corner of the sofa to snuggle on, I stopped. Because slumped on it already was Claire with Franceska, who was hugging her as she cried.

I felt my heart sink, as I fretted for another person I loved. As one problem was solved, another presented itself. That was how it seemed to be with humans, or the ones in my life anyway.

-CHAPTER-

Fifteen

'Claire, is going to be OK,' Franceska said, stroking her hair, the way I had seen her do with her boys when they were upset. Whenever Franceska was stressed her accent was stronger and the way she spoke reminded me of when she first arrived in Edgar Road.

I was confused and scared. When I got up this morning, Claire had seemed fine. She fed me, got ready for work and left the house at the same time as Jonathan, in a puff of smiles and kisses. But now she was wearing what looked like her bed clothes, and her face was red and puffy.

'I'm sorry, Frankie but I was so sure, and then this,' she sobbed noisily.

'Claire, sweetie, you must stay calm. This doesn't help, and I know everyone says it but you have time, it's not a rush.'

'I know, but I can't help how I feel. I really thought I was pregnant, my period was late, I really felt it, and then today at work, I get the crushing period pains. I'm sorry, Frankie, I know I'm not being sane but I just feel as if I'm going mad.'

'How long have you been trying?'

'Over eight months now.'

'Is nothing. It took me a year to get pregnant with Aleksy.' Franceska was still stroking her hair, and I hung back. I didn't want to intrude or interrupt.

'Really?' Claire looked up with teary eyes. 'I guess I am being silly but you know, I'm nearly forty and I know that it's not too old but I want us to be a family so much. I couldn't believe it, after the divorce, that I got together with Jonathan and we have such an amazing life. But then I see your boys and Polly … and I really want that. I'm desperate for it.'

'And you will have it, but you need to stop crying, and relax. I am sure everyone is saying it but you enjoy trying and it will happen.'

'I don't want Jonathan to see me like this. It's not that I'm trying to hide from him but he tries so hard to protect me from feeling bad again. After I told him everything about my divorce and then my disastrous relationship with Joe, he has been so good at looking after me, and I don't want to worry him.'

'Right, then I shall make you a coffee, you will clean that face and when he comes from work you tell him you're a bit unwell, and then rest. That way he can take care of you without the worry so much.'

'Oh, Frankie, where would I be without you?'

I decided it was time to make my presence known, so I miaowed.

'Alfie, I didn't know you were here,' Claire said, furiously rubbing her eyes. I jumped up onto her lap and snuggled into her neck. She rubbed the top of my head, my favourite spot and then I went to say hello to Franceska.

'OK, I make some drinks for us and get Alfie a snack, OK?'

'Great, thank you, Frankie.'

I almost glued myself to Franceska's leg as she went to the kitchen. I didn't want to take any chances when it came to getting fed, so I jumped up on the kitchen counter and pointed my nose in the direction of the cupboard where they kept the tuna. I stood on my hind legs and scratched at the cupboard door, and although I couldn't open it, it was enough to alert Franceska as to what I wanted. I wasn't being greedy but the emotion of the day had left me feeling hungry.

'Ah, Alfie, calm down, I get you some!' She pulled out a tin of tuna, opened it and tipped it in my bowl. She then got me some milk. I purred in thanks as I got stuck in.

Before Franceska left she made a hot water bottle for Claire and sent her to bed. I thought about joining her but as I had so much to think about I decided to stay downstairs, and go back to my original plan of trying to get my head straight. Only now I had even more to think about, because my list was once again growing. Tiger, Snowball and her family and now Claire. There was too much going on for me to process, especially as I now had a full tummy. So with my head full of thoughts, sunlight flowing through the window, I curled up on the sofa and fell into a lovely sleep.

I woke, it must have been hours later, because I heard Jonathan's key in the door. I stretched my legs out sleepily and jumped off the sofa to greet him.

'Hey, Alfie.' He threw his keys onto the side table and bent down to pet me. I purred and offered him my paw for our customary high five. 'Right, I'd better go and see our patient.' He kicked off his shoes and ran upstairs. I followed him, running as fast as I could to keep up. He opened the bedroom door and went in, where I could see Claire sitting up in bed and reading. She looked far more composed now than the last time I saw her.

'Hi, darling, are you all right?' Jonathan went up to her and kissed her head.

'Hey, I'm feeling a bit better, just really bad stomach pains, you know, time of the month.' She smiled though and although I saw a flicker of something in Jonathan's eyes he seemed to quickly recover.

'In that case, I shall go to the gym and then on the way back pick us up a take-away. What do you fancy?'

'Thai.' Claire grinned and I felt relieved as I jumped up onto the bed next to her. 'I might have pains, but I'm so hungry.'

'Thai it is then, my love. Right, I'd better get going.' He kissed her again, gave me a rough head scratch and then went to get changed into his gym kit. I was satisfied that Claire was all right, or at least she was for now, I thought, as I got down from the bed and went downstairs. As I made my way out of the cat flap, I started following my sense of smell. It was time for me to go and make amends with one of the other women in my life: Tiger.

I hadn't had much time to think about what Rocky had said, but I decided that for now I would just ensure our friendship wasn't damaged. I wasn't exactly sure how to sort this situation out – I had never been in love before like this and I had never had anyone in love with me the way Rocky said Tiger was – I had to tread carefully. In the meantime I would ensure that Tiger knew she was important to me, in a friendship way of course.

I quickly located my friend. It wasn't hard, given that she was at home eating her supper. I put my head gently through the cat flap to see if the coast was clear. Seeing that it was, I hissed gently to her and she turned around and saw me. She must have forgotten to be cross as, for a second, she looked pleased to see me until she remembered and scowled at me.

'Can you come out here?' I asked. I couldn't go inside and risk seeing her family. They didn't like other cats in their house.

'I'm having my dinner. I shall come out when I'm finished,' she said in a hoity-toity voice. I didn't answer, but I gave her my most charming look and popped my head back out. I sat patiently by the rose bush as I waited for Tiger to appear. I knew deep down that she would take her time. And boy did she.

'I've almost forgotten why I came here,' I said as she appeared sometime later.

'Alfie, the world doesn't revolve around you.'

'I know, I know.' I was the sort of cat that spent most of his time worrying about others, but it wasn't the time to point that out to Tiger. Not when she was in one of her moods. I remembered Rocky's words and realized that perhaps I had been remiss in reading the signs. She really did seem very angry with me.

I thought back to when I first met her. We had become firm friends and had a happy relationship. She was definitely my best cat friend and I'd do anything for her. She was protective towards me, like when she came to Aleksy's school, she looked out for me; but things had changed slightly, and maybe I had failed to notice the shift in our relationship. I didn't understand why she seemed so stroppy with me these days.

'It's frustrating sometimes, Alfie,' she said, sounding sad.

'But I would never do anything to upset you on purpose, you know that don't you?' I said, looking at her. She cocked her head to one side.

'I hope so,' she said sadly. I was none the wiser as to why she was actually upset but I was sorry that I'd made her sad.

'I know, let's go to the park and look at the moon in the water,' I suggested in an attempt to diffuse the situation.

'Wow, you must be sorry,' she said. It was true. Tiger loved to go to the pond and stare at the moon's reflection in the water. She put her face too close to it and it terrified me, after my near-drowning experience. So on the rare occasion

I would go with her I kept well back. Now I wanted to show her how much her friendship meant to me and overcoming my fear and looking at the moon seemed appropriate.

We walked along in silence, passing hedges and garden gates but not stopping to look at other houses. I was focusing all my attention on Tiger. When we reached the park it seemed deserted. I could hear signs of other animals but they were keeping well hidden in the darkness. We made our way to the pond and I took a deep breath, as Tiger bounded to the water's edge and I made my way there carefully.

'My favourite is the round moon,' Tiger said as she looked at the big round ball which seemed to glimmer as it floated on the water's surface.

'It is beautiful,' I agreed as I stood perilously close to the water's edge and opened one eye to see the moon while keeping the other closed. I felt my legs shaking and I tried very hard to be brave but I seemed to fail.

'Oh, Alfie, you're petrified! But I appreciate you doing this for me.' Tiger laughed kindly, and we thankfully moved away from the pond.

'I'm sorry we fought,' I said. 'I hate it when that happens.'

'I know and I get it that you're infatuated with that white cat and her bloody family.'

'I don't meant to be,' I offered.

'You never do. But you can't help yourself, Alfie. It's always like you have to fix things and when there isn't anything to fix you almost go looking for stuff.'

'I do, don't I?'

'Even in the last couple of years when the families all seemed happy, you have been worrying about the children, and Polly, and of course Claire and Jonathan, it's just what you do.'

'I can't help it, it's as if finding Edgar Road and being given my second chance at happiness came with a need for me to help people.' I sighed; it was tiring worrying so much but there seemed no alternative at times. Tiger sighed too.

'It's why I care about you and get mad at you all at the same time. Come on then, I guess you're dying to tell me what happened at Snowball's this morning.' Tiger looked a bit embarrassed but I was happy to fill her in. It felt like safer ground.

I couldn't believe I had forgotten about it. It seemed so long ago and so much had happened in that time. So as we started to make our way back home, wrapped in the darkness of night, I started to tell Tiger about my encounter with Daisy and then Snowball and I felt something shifting inside. Tiger and I might not be completely on the same page but our friendship was stronger than ever, I was sure of that.

As we stopped outside the Goodwins' house we couldn't resist jumping up on their garden wall. For once Heather and Vic weren't at the window but Salmon was. We started taunting him, safe in the knowledge that if he did try to come outside we'd be long gone by the time he made it. Tiger and I grinned at each other as Salmon snarled like a dog, flicked his tail and bared his teeth at us. We teased a while longer and then jumped down and headed home. We strolled back shoulder to shoulder and it seemed that all had been forgiven. I decided I needed to put what Rocky said about Tiger to the back of my mind. I had a list as long as my tail of people who needed my help, and I wouldn't rest until I'd done what I needed to do.

CHAPTER

Sixteen

I spotted Polly a while before she saw me. She was on her own, walking back to the house with a couple of shopping bags, humming to herself. At the same time, I noticed the front door of Snowball's house open a crack, and I saw my chance. I rushed forth, so when Polly reached their gate, I stood in front of her, stopping her in her tracks, in the hope of engineering a meeting. Polly bent down to pet me as the front door opened and the mother, Karen, appeared. She was wearing a pair of jeans and a shirt and she looked uncertainly around her as she made her way out of the house and up to the front gate.

'Oh,' she said startled as she spotted us. She had dark rings under her eyes and she looked a bit messy. Or not exactly well-groomed like me, anyway. I never left the house with any fur out of place. Looking my best was incredibly important to me.

'Hi, I'm Polly.' Polly adjusted her bags and held out her hand. Karen looked at it as if she had never seen a hand before in her life. She went to take it and then she burst into tears. Polly and I were both taken aback.

'I'm Karen,' she sobbed.

'Hey,' Polly said in her gentle voice that always soothed me. 'What's wrong?'

'I can't, I can't talk here,' Karen said, she looked directly across the road to Heather and Vic's house.

Polly nodded. 'Listen, my house is only a few doors away, and my husband has taken the kids out, so it's empty if you fancy a cuppa?'

'I really shouldn't,' Karen protested.

'It can't hurt can it? Karen, you clearly need some time to collect yourself. Come on.' Polly looked determined, like a woman who wouldn't take no for an answer. And this cat wouldn't either, as I decided to tag along with them.

Karen was quite a lot shorter than Polly, although most women were. She was about the same height as Franceska, her muddy blonde hair tied back in a ponytail. While Polly walked tall, holding herself with confidence and grace, Karen was walking as if she was shrinking into herself with each step. I could almost feel her weightiness; she walked as if she carried a whole other person on her back.

I don't think she even noticed me as I padded along a couple of steps behind them, determined not to miss this opportunity.

Polly opened the door and silence greeted us, a rare event in Polly's house. It made me laugh, because Polly was like an excited kid when no one else was around (apart from me), and once alone she would kick her shoes off, grab a bar of chocolate from her secret stash, put on a face pack, watch TV programmes she told me Matt hated or read her stack of magazines. Although not today of course, as Karen followed her into their small homely kitchen, and sat at the table as Polly wordlessly went to switch on the kettle.

'Sorry,' Karen started. 'I shouldn't be here.'

'Why ever not?' Polly asked. 'Look, love, it's OK to chat to me, you know.'

'It's not that, it's just we agreed. No one else needs to know our business, not after what happened.'

'OK, but if you do want to talk, I'm quite friendly.' Polly smiled, then busied herself pouring tea before sitting opposite Karen.

'Please, I can't go into it now. But it doesn't help that *those* people think we're criminals.'

'Oh, you must mean the Goodwins. I wouldn't worry about them; they're just the street busybodies.'

'They keep coming round, knocking on our door, normally when I am at work but it's driving Tim – that's my husband – crazy. I told him that he should maybe answer the door to them, and put a stop to it, but he won't.'

'Well I guess they're surprised that you haven't been to one of their Neighbourhood Watch meetings,' Polly said. 'This is such a big street, but they kind of rule this part of it, unfortunately.' Polly attempted a laugh, but it sounded wrong.

'We couldn't face it. Not yet, I'm not sure ever. All the questions. Tim saw them spying on us when the police came round the other day, they would want to know everything and I can't answer those questions.' Karen seemed slightly hysterical and I thought I understood now why Snowball was so hostile; she obviously had a lot on her plate.

'I know they are way too interested in everything that's going on, but I guess that by ignoring them you are fuelling that curiosity,' Polly said, tentatively.

'Polly, we aren't criminals.'

'Oh no, I wasn't implying that, love.'

'We're just a family, having a tough time and want to be left alone.'

'Yet you're sitting here with me. It can be lonely cutting yourself off – I should know, I've been there. We only want to help though.'

'Yes.' Karen looked as if she remembered that she was indeed doing that. I sat under the table, and listened, I didn't want to draw attention to myself. 'And I'm sorry, I don't mean to be rude, it's just that, well, I guess I'm not ready to be around people just yet. I'm so tired, working all hours, it's not that I want to be anti-social, but we just need a bit of space.'

'Hey, whatever you need.' Polly tried to look supportive but I could see her underlying confusion. She didn't look as if she knew what was going on and neither did I.

'I had a row with my son, Christopher. He's fourteen and so angry all the time.'

'Hormonal teenager?'

'Yes, but more than that. My poor children have been through so much… I really am sorry to be so weird but I just–'

'Hey.' Polly held her hands up in defeat. 'Honestly, as long as you're OK. And you know where I am if you ever do want to talk. I'd hate you to think we're all like Heather and Vic.' Polly, was full of compassion, it was one of the things all my families had in common.

Karen stood up. 'I'm sorry again, but I really must go.' Karen went to the front door, said a distracted goodbye and, looking around furtively, hurried off down the street.

'Well for someone who has nothing to hide she sure acts like she does,' Polly said as she picked me up and started stroking my fur. 'I mean, Alfie, I'm sure there's nothing criminal about them but she clearly isn't the most normal person I've ever met.' I miaowed my agreement. It seemed none of the family could give a straight answer. They all talked in riddles, never letting their guard down about whatever secret it was they were hiding. None of us had any idea what was going on.

My only conclusion was that if they didn't have anything to hide, they were hiding from something. Or someone. Or everyone for that matter.

★★★

A little while later, the door opened as Polly and I sat side by side on her sofa, her flicking through magazines, me processing my thoughts. With a thundering of little feet, Henry ran in.

'Mummy! We saw a rabbit, and some cows. Alfie! Hi, Alfie.' I loved Henry's excitement.

'Where on earth did you take them?' Polly asked, when Matt came in.

'To the toy shop,' he laughed. 'They had a farm set and Henry spent ages playing with it, he loved it. I told him we'd get him some animals for his birthday.'

'And where is my little girl?' Polly said as Henry climbed on his mum and smothered her with cuddles.

'Asleep in the pushchair. Hi, Alfie.' Matt sat down, so we were all squished together on their sofa.

'We need a bigger sofa,' Polly observed.

'Or maybe this boy could take up less room,' he replied, tickling Henry so he giggled and wriggled.

'Oh, Daddy.' Henry laughed.

'By the way, I bumped into the lady from number forty-eight today, Karen. She was upset so I invited her round and although she came she was still so secretive and basically couldn't wait to leave. I have no idea what's going on. I don't think they're a danger to the road like some think, but I agree that it is strange.'

'Yeah, that's what Jonathan said. He said they acted like everyone was out to get them.'

'Actually that's it, that's exactly what it was like.'

'But the Goodwins aren't helping,' Matt said. 'They're fixated on them; it's like an obsession.'

'Well maybe if we can get the Goodwins off their back they might start to behave a bit more normally then.'

'You got any ideas how to stop Heather and Vic?' Matt asked with a grin.

'Short of locking them up, no.' Polly laughed. 'But remember how sad I was when I moved here. When Frankie tried to be friendly to me I pushed her away. What if it's like that?'

'Oh, darling, you weren't well then and maybe they have their own problems, but unless they want to tell us we can't make them.'

'No, Matt, we can't but putting the brakes on the Goodwins would be a good start.' She looked determined.

I miaowed loudly. Polly and I were the most in tune it seemed, at the moment anyway. She was right, if the newcomers weren't ready to tell us what was going on, then we needed to get the Goodwins to back off and then hopefully they might feel a bit more welcome, until they were ready to open up. That was what we had to do but I had no idea how we would do it. Once again I had to put my thinking cap on and let the head scratching – although I actually did enjoy a little head scratch – ensue.

-CHAPTER-
Seventeen

I trembled at the sight of cat carrier; normally it heralded a trip to the vet, which never ended well. It was four days after I'd met Karen, and the weekend was looming. Claire had also put my cat bed by the front door, along with a bag of cat food. My eyes widened; was I being given away? I couldn't think of anything I had done wrong, although yesterday I had been looking through the fence at next door in the hope of seeing Snowball and I'd come nose to nose with an annoying little mouse. It had been so scared that the stupid thing ran towards me and into my garden. I was actually trying to get rid of it, but somehow – probably due to what Tiger called my inept hunting technique – the mouse had ended up in my house. As it ran off I was going to get it but then I was distracted by a lovely smell, and forgot all about it. Instead, I'd sniffed the fresh laundry that sat in the basket waiting to be put away, before noticing that on top was my favourite – Jonathan's favourite – cashmere jumper. It had seemed so delicious and was so soft that I couldn't resist jumping on it and, before I knew it, I'd fallen asleep.

A commotion had woken me; all hell had broken loose. Claire was screaming and standing on a chair in the kitchen. Jonathan was running around with a broom and when I emerged, they both looked at me in an accusatory way.

'Did you bring a mouse in?' Claire asked, sounding annoyed. I miaowed, realizing I'd forgotten about it. But in my defence, I then sniffed it out and chased it back into the garden. But then Jonathan picked up his jumper.

'You've been sleeping on my best jumper!' he shouted, clearly unhappy. 'Look it's covered in your fur, Alfie, how many times do I have to tell you to keep away from my cashmere?' he stormed. Claire and he were clearly unhappy with me and now, looking at the cat carrier, it seemed they were punishing me in the worst way.

'Ready for your holiday?' she asked me, picking me up. I looked at her, head cocked to one side. 'Remember I told you that Jon and I were going away this weekend, so you're going to stay with Franceska and the boys.' A feeling of relief flooded me and I breathed again. Ahh, of course! I'd forgotten. Jonathan had booked a weekend away for them, somewhere called Paris which was in a different country apparently, and they were going for three days. I would normally stay at Polly and Matt's but this time, Franceska was going to take me to Aleksy's school to see the Alfie project, after spending the weekend with them.

Although I was going to stay with people I loved, I wondered how I would cope being so far from my street. I was nervous away from Edgar Road, and felt trepidation of places unknown. I had learnt that adventure wasn't always a good thing and actually quite a lot of it for me had been bad. I shuddered and my fur stood on end as some of the memories flooded my head. As I started to scramble out of Claire's arms and away from the cat carrier, I realized I needed to calm down, reminding myself that I had been to Franceska's before, so it wasn't like going to the unknown.

I did have to give myself a talking to quite often. Memories of my journey to Edgar Road still invoked terror in me. It was sometimes hard to remember that I was safe and loved although I constantly tried to remind myself.

'Don't be such a silly cat,' Claire said, coming towards me and stroking my fur. 'You're going to have so much fun, Alfie, and hopefully so will we. I'll pick you up on Monday evening.' She kissed the tip of my nose and put me down on the floor. Although I hated being in the cage, I knew there was no option, and the idea of a few days with Aleksy and the others couldn't help but make me smile. And of course, I was expecting gourmet sardines from my lovely Franceska. So, as I talked myself down I remembered that I would actually have a lovely time. Yes, I would enjoy my holiday. Although I would miss trying to catch a glimpse of Snowball.

Claire drove me to my holiday home, all the while chatting animatedly about how much she was looking forward to going away with Jonathan. Of every human I knew, I loved it that Claire still talked to me the most. I guess it was a habit she had developed when we lived together, just the two of us, before she moved in with Jonathan.

By the time Claire found a parking space on Franceska's road, I knew that she was hoping that this weekend, spent in a luxury hotel, would result in her being pregnant. I basked in happiness when Claire was like this – she had her dark moments, but who doesn't? Claire's had the potential to be worse than most though and I fervently hoped she would get what she wanted. Not only was I happy to have an addition to our family but I wanted that happiness to last. I always worried that it wouldn't.

Happiness was so wonderful but it could also be scarily fickle.

HAPPY HOLIDAY ALFIE! greeted me. Aleksy had made me a banner painted in rainbow colours along with a picture of me. Aleksy looked both proud and a little shy as everyone praised his artistic talents. I miaowed and jumped up into his arms – it was our new favourite trick. Aleksy thought he'd taught me but we all know who the teacher was really.

As everyone clapped and grinned I felt as if I had come home again. I did miss this lovely family who meant so much to me and although they had travelled further than I had to get to Edgar Road all that time ago, we still would always share that bond. They were immigrants, Tomasz used to tell me, which meant they weren't born in this country. But they worked hard and were such good people that I knew that they actually belonged here now, with me. Or I belonged with them.

As Claire and Franceska went to the kitchen to have a chat, Tomasz and Aleksy took me into their living room where I was presented with a lot of toys all laid out for me. It was playtime.

After chasing fake mice, cars, and running around in circles, I collapsed on my back and let the boys tickle and fuss over me. I was tired but very happy as Claire came in to say goodbye. She gave me a huge cuddle and kiss and told me to be good – as if I would be anything but – and then she left.

'Right, Alfie, is your dinner time?' Franceska asked.

'Can I feed him?' little Tomasz asked. I followed them to the kitchen where Franceska made me a very happy cat by getting a tin of sardines out of the cupboard. I tried to be patient as Tomasz helped open the tin and with 'careful, careful' repeated, he tipped the sardines in my bowl.

I eagerly got stuck in when they were finally put on the floor and Tomasz stood by proudly as I ate. My boys were growing up fast. When I first met Tomasz he was still very small, taking naps and learning to talk. Now he and Aleksy were like proper little people.

The door flew open and I heard the booming voice of big

Tomasz, their father. He came into the kitchen carrying cartons of food. Aleksy came running into the kitchen after him.

'Pappa,' little Tomasz shouted, gleefully.

'Dinner,' big Tomasz said, putting the food on the counter. He scooped up both of his children into a big hug, they all laughed. Tomasz was a big man and towered over his wife as he kissed her. 'Ah and here is our guest. Welcome to our little home, Alfie,' he said, picking me up and stroking me. I purred into his massive neck.

'How long can you stay?' Franceska asked.

'We are fully booked tonight, so I have to go back in an hour.'

'Right, better get this heated up quickly then.' She smiled.

'I'm sorry, *kochanie*, I will get back as early as possible.'

'I know, but now it's getting so busy, which is good, can you get more staff?'

'We are trying, I promise, but it's difficult to find good staff. I have more interviews next week, so fingers crossed.'

'Good, because I love you work so hard for us but it would be nice to see you a bit more.' Franceska smiled, though, and I knew she wasn't really angry, I just wondered if she was a bit lonely while her husband worked so much.

Later that afternoon, I stood by the flat door and miaowed. I wanted to go out, but there was no cat flap in the second floor flat, and although they had got me a litter tray I turned my nose up at it. I would use it in emergencies but I didn't want to if I didn't have to. I wasn't that sort of cat.

Franceska, gestured to me to follow her and she opened a back door, which I hadn't noticed before, and she walked with me down a flight of stairs. We emerged into a small yard.

'This is the back of the restaurant, I can leave the door open for you, but be quick as I don't want any mice to get in,' she said.

I was pleased by this limited freedom and I found a patch of weeds to do my business in, before quickly scoping out my surroundings. There were some big bins in a small-ish yard which led to an alley. My nose was aroused, I could smell wildlife here, mice and even those horrible big rats. But then it made sense. Where there was rubbish, there was vermin. I didn't need Franceska to tell me to be quick; I wasn't sure I fancied hanging around here too long. Although I didn't catch sight of anything, I knew they were lurking in the shadows waiting for scraps to feed off.

I bounded back upstairs and Franceska went down to close the door. She looked relieved when we were back inside.

'I just don't want any of those mice or rats coming in here,' she said, as Aleksy and Tomasz sat on the sofa, in their pyjamas, watching television. 'Hazard of living above a restaurant,' she explained. I tilted my head in sympathy. It wasn't nice. And of course although I could see off a few mice, I tended to avoid rats, some of whom seemed almost as big as me.

'But what about Dustbin?' Aleksy said.

'Oh yes, he is very good at catching them, but they still seem to come back.' I miaowed, wanting them to tell me who Dustbin was. They looked at me and laughed.

'Dustbin is a cat who lives by the dustbins. I'm surprised you didn't see him just then. He gets fed by the restaurant and he chases off the mice and rats. He's a big cat.'

'He is much bigger than you, Alfie, and he never goes inside, ever,' Aleksy explained.

I was curious and wondered if I would meet this cat while I was staying.

'He smells funny,' Tomasz piped up. 'And his fur is very messy, not like yours.' I was a silver/grey coloured cat, with a tinge of blue in my fur, my eyes were shiny and healthy and my perfectly round face was proportionate to my slender body.

'Yes, it is true he is not as good-looking as Alfie,' Franceska concurred. My fur gleamed in pride. 'But he is a good cat nonetheless and we don't need to be mean about him.'

'Oh no, Mamma, I like him,' Tomasz added, giggling. 'He's not a house cat like Alfie but he is a cat.'

'Of course he's a cat, dummy, you get different kinds of cats,' Aleksy said. I smiled through my whiskers. Aleksy was right, you get different kinds of cats and different kinds of people. It was how the world worked.

Later that night I woke, briefly wondering where I was. I knew I was in my bed, but, as I blinked through the darkness I could see two beds, one with Aleksy sleeping, his covers all thrown off him and a leg hanging over the side, and Tomasz, still fully tucked in. Franceska had talked about how Aleksy loved school again now since the bullying incident which seemed to be firmly behind him. And she credited me with being the one who saved the day. I smiled as I remembered that I was on something called a 'holiday' with some of my favourite people, so I settled back down and managed to drift back to sleep. After all, holidays were for taking it easy, and I intended to do just that.

-CHAPTER-
Eighteen

I had developed a compulsive need to meet this cat called Dustbin, due to the fact that he was obviously part of my Polish family's life. I was let out into the back yard after breakfast but there was no sign of him, just a few dirty mice scratching around. They looked startled to see me but I wasn't interested in them, having enjoyed a hearty breakfast. I could see a way out of the yard, which seemed to lead to an alleyway but I was reluctant to explore the unknown territory. I returned with my curiosity far from sated as we spent the morning at home in the flat. Big Tomasz had the morning off, and while Franceska went to the shops, us boys played video games. I tried to join in, watching a bird flying around on screen which I tried to follow with my paw, but I lost my normally incredible balance and fell off the TV stand. The boys shrieked with laughter. Slightly humiliated I then tried to see if I could use the controllers they were holding onto but they kept swerving them out of my grasp. In the end I gave up and became a spectator.

'Alfie, we are going to take Aleksy to football this afternoon,' big Tomasz said, as Franceska returned and called the boys in for lunch. I joined them, although I wasn't expecting any food, I liked being around the action.

'Can Alfie come?' Aleksy asked, excitedly, and I purred and jumped into Tomasz's arms. I had no real idea what they meant but I wanted to go to wherever it was.

I cried to be let out again, as the family sat down for lunch and as I stepped out the door I immediately struck gold as I met the cat that could only be Dustbin. He was a little fragrant, I have to admit (and not in a good way), and his fur stuck up in all directions; he was also huge, almost as big as a dog. As I stood stock still, unsure of the reception I could expect, he turned to me.

'Hello, who are you?' he asked, not unkindly.

'I'm Alfie. I'm staying upstairs for a few days.'

'Ah, with big Tomasz. I'm Dustbin. Not my real name. Not sure what my real name is to be honest. I was given this name by the family upstairs and well, it's as good as any.' Although he was clearly feral, he was very polite.

'I'm not trying to encroach on your territory,' I said quickly. He waved a paw at me.

'Hadn't crossed my mind and anyway I'm happy to share.' He smiled, and I saw his teeth were pretty sharp, I was thankful that he wasn't angry with me. Or inclined to eat me.

'I live where they used to live, and my other family are away. Nice to meet you.'

'Nice to meet you too, Alfie. I guess you get a bit pampered?'

'I do,' I admitted. 'I was homeless, a street cat for a while though, and I have to say I don't know how you do it. I like hot fires, warm laps, and food served to me in bowls.' I smiled and Dustbin laughed.

'Well it takes all sorts. I mean your life sounds pretty nice, but not for me. I like the freedom, and I have food on tap here. As long as I keep the mice and rat population down, I get fed pretty well from the restaurant too.'

'But the cold?'

'You get used to it. There is plenty of shelter here and I like being my own man.'

'Don't you get lonely?' I asked.

'I have friends, well, sort of. There are a group of us round here, all outdoor cats, so it's not so bad.' He chuckled. I couldn't contemplate having his life, but it made me feel a bit of a pampered cat.

'Alfie,' I heard Franceska call from upstairs, before I could pursue the conversation further.

'I'd better go, but I'll be back later. It'd be nice to see you again.'

'Sure, you too. See you later.'

As I ran back upstairs I thought what a nice cat Dustbin was. A little bit wild but really very friendly. As he said, it took all sorts. Life would be pretty boring if we were all the same. That applied to humans and cats alike.

Big Tomasz carried me to football. They were worried about losing me he said, so he tucked me neatly under his arm and we walked past the school and towards a big field. Aleksy was wearing baggy shorts and a shirt with a number on the back, and he was bouncing with excitement.

'Don't use all your energy before you get on the field,' his dad said. Franceska laughed as she held onto little Tomasz's hand. I was almost as excited as Aleksy, although I had no idea what to expect.

When we reached the field, there were lots of children and adults already there, standing around. A man blew a whistle and all the children rushed onto the pitch.

'Good luck, Aleksy,' my family shouted. He turned back, smiled and waved.

Tomasz kept hold of me which I was grateful for because there were lots of people and it was also quite cold. I snuggled into Tomasz's jacket as the match began. I knew all about football from watching it with Jonathan and Matt, but I had never seen it played live. And I had never seen children play before. Which quickly turned out to be a good thing.

When they started playing, it was a little bit of a mess. No one seemed to know which way to run, and although the adults were cheering and shouting, there was no clear sense to what everyone was doing. The ball flew past me as a child fell over trying to kick it. Franceska and Tomasz laughed and little Tomasz clapped his hands. Other people were shouting, and I noticed that some weren't finding it funny, but these kids were certainly energetic even if none of them were any good at actually playing football. A whistle blew and Aleksy ran over to us with most of his team.

'Aleksy,' Tomasz admonished. 'You are supposed to talk to your coach not come over to us.'

'But, Pappa, I wanted to show Alfie to the team.' The children, who were wearing the same shirts as Aleksy, all crowded around me and some reached to stroke me. I noticed there was boys and girls in the team, and some I recognized from my visit to the school. They seemed almost as enthusiastic about seeing me as they were about the game. As the children cooed over me, a tubby man came over to us.

'Hello, Mr Armstrong,' Franceska said.

'Hi.' He looked a bit sheepish as he interrupted the goings on, and I guessed he was in charge. 'Come on, you lot, it's nearly time for the second half.' He nodded seriously at Tomasz and Franceska. 'What are you all doing anyway?'

'It's Alfie, our cat,' Aleksy explained. 'He has come to see us play and is our lucky mascot.' Aleksy puffed out his chest proudly, and I did the same. Although I didn't seem to have proved lucky so far as no one had scored any goals.

'OK, well, Alfie, perhaps you can bring us some goals in the second half,' Mr Armstrong jested. I miaowed in response; I didn't know how, after all it didn't seem they were going to let me play.

Somehow I became a hero with Aleksy's friends yet again. I even noticed that the bully was playing and although he hung back from me, Aleksy and he seemed to be friendly as they stood side by side on the football pitch. So when Aleksy scored a goal, the crowd cheered loudly; big Tomasz jumped up with me almost flying out of his arms; Franceska squealed; little Tomasz cheered and clapped his hands; and I grinned my biggest grin. When a little girl on Aleksy's team scored a second goal just before the final whistle went, they all ran over to me and gave me credit for the win.

I loved being a cat sometimes; I didn't have to do anything and yet I was always getting praised.

On Sunday the restaurant was closed, so Tomasz took us all down there.

'Alfie hasn't seen it yet and although I know no animals are allowed, no one will know.' He winked at Franceska.

'He can go and play in the yard with Dustbin,' she said. As they started doing stuff in the restaurant the boys came outside with me where they greeted Dustbin like an old friend, as did I. Obviously I couldn't speak to him properly with the boys there but when they were called in to do their homework, we got to hang out.

'So you've had a nice weekend?' Dustbin asked.

'Actually, I have. I went to see Aleksy play football yesterday, and tomorrow, before I go home, I'm going to the school for a visit.'

'You do have an interesting life,' he said.

'Well I seem to have a few adventures. But when I was homeless I was so miserable, and I really feared for my life. Sometimes even now I wonder how I survived. I guess I'm lucky to have such caring people around me.'

'You are, but then I've always been a street cat and I wouldn't fare well in a home. Franceska suggested to Tomasz that they take me in but I would have hated that. Especially as it apparently involved getting me bathed and taken to a vet!'

'Trust me, I've been through both and neither are fun,' I replied sagely.

'I'm not cut out for domesticity. I mean I like the boys well enough, but I wouldn't want to have to play with them too often.' He laughed. 'I like the freedom that this life gives me.'

'So it's your choice?' I asked.

'I'm not sure I'd call it choice, exactly.' He looked thoughtful. 'I was born into it and I just got used to it. Tomasz keeps me well fed and I keep down the vermin around here. It's like a job really.'

'When I was homeless I saw some people who lived on the streets. But they were drunk and mean to me. I met street cats too, and some of them scared me, but one of them was really great.'

'And not all people who live on the street are drunks. Remember, this world is far from perfect; yours might be but others aren't so fortunate. I know many people who live outside because they don't have a choice, not because they like it, and it's very sad.'

'There's so much I don't know about the world still, I guess,' I admitted.

'There's so much we all don't know, but hey, Alfie, just

appreciate all you have, and take care of the people who love you.'

'I will, Dustbin. I wish we had more time together but if I come back again I hope to see you.'

'You too, Alfie, I might teach you effective hunting,' he laughed.

'My friend Tiger would tell you that I'm the worse hunter ever.' I tried though, as I followed Dustbin around the yard. Unfortunately I lived up to my reputation. I swiped for one mouse who darted out of my grasp, and I spun round to find it, tripped over my tail and ended up on my bottom. Not to be deterred, I stalked another mouse, but I pounced a bit too soon and the mouse sprang out of my loose lips and bit me on the nose.

'Ow,' I cried, dropping it on its head. Dustbin was almost crying with laughter and I decided to quit while I just had a slightly sore nose and bruised pride.

We waved our tails in a friendly goodbye and I thought what an interesting cat he was.

CHAPTER

Nineteen

Today was the day that I was going to school with Aleksy. We were all incredibly excited. Apart from little Tomasz who was annoyed that I wasn't going to his class.

'It's not fair,' he whined.

'Don't sound like a baby, Tomasz. Your class hasn't done an Alfie project; maybe some other time,' Franceska chastised. Little Tomasz crossed his arms over his chest and stuck his bottom lip out. I went up to him and tickled him with my tail, which I knew would get him. He laughed and then he picked me up and gave me a cuddle. Tomasz was still only five but he was big for his age. Jonathan called him 'a bruiser,' which seemed to suit him.

'So, if Alfie can't come to my class then can I carry him to school?' he asked.

'OK, but I'll bring the carrier in case you get tired,' Franceska replied. Great, I was going to be caged again. I definitely wasn't looking forward to that part of the day.

But even that couldn't dampen my spirits. I couldn't wait to tell Tiger all about it.

I felt a pang. I had barely given her a thought since I'd been on my holiday. I had, of course, thought a lot about Snowball; she was the last thing on my mind before I went to sleep and the first thing I thought of on waking. I felt guilty about Tiger but then what could I do? I missed everyone from Edgar Road, but I missed seeing Snowball the most. A cat I had only known for just over two months. What did that say about me?

Once the boys were dressed in their school uniforms, I

was put into the cat carrier by Aleksy. He looked as if he was beside himself with excitement as his eyes shone and he kept hopping from foot to foot.

'Aleksy, I wish you were always so keen to go to school,' Franceska teased.

'Maybe I would be if Alfie came with me every day,' he replied, cheekily. I miaowed loudly. There was no way I could go to school every day; I was far too busy.

Excitedly, I realized that being the hero of the football match would have increased my already great popularity at school. It was lucky I wasn't a big headed cat; I knew it was just the affection of children, and I tried not to get too proud. It really was a very nice feeling though.

Franceska dropped Tomasz, who was carrying me, at his classroom, wrestling me from him, and we then went to Aleksy's class, where everyone was waiting. As the children crowded round me, still in Franceska's arms, the teacher, the pretty Miss Walton, who had gently ejected me from her class-room last time, welcomed me warmly. She put me on her desk and all the children came to see me one by one. They were all gentle, even the bully who seemed to have changed his ways.

Eventually, everyone was told to settle down, and Franceska left the classroom. I took the opportunity for a good look around. On my first visit, I had been so preoccupied with Aleksy and the missing Molly that I hadn't properly noticed the surroundings. A big white board was at the front of the room, and desks were lined up with bright plastic chairs. Paintings covered most of the walls and there was a book corner where there were more books than I had ever seen. At the back of the room a hamster was eyeing me suspiciously from its cage. It was a bright, colourful room and I felt pleased as punch to be there again.

Then the children all read out parts of a story they had written about me. It was about a cat, called Alfie (naturally), who had magic powers. The cat could stop people being sad and from being hurt; basically, he could solve any school problems or home issues. When Aleksy read out his bit it said this magic cat taught children to be good children. It was actually quite an emotional story and although not all of it made sense – cats cannot fly through the air and we don't wear capes – I felt a bit choked up by the time the story came to the end.

I miaowed loudly to show my approval which made everyone laugh. The teacher picked me up to view the childrens' paintings of me, which adorned the classroom wall. As I looked at them all, I admit I preened a bit. I felt very special and very lucky, and suddenly I realized how far I had come from being a homeless cat with no one to love him.

Miss Walton carried me out to Franceska when the stories had been read and the children said a reluctant goodbye to me. I was a little hurt to be bundled, yet again, into the cat carrier.

After being released from my jail back at the flat, it was just me and Franceska for the first time in ages. As Franceska and I shared a special bond, I was happy for our rare time together. She took her jacket off, and let me out of the carrier. I followed her into the kitchen where she put the kettle on and then put some milk in a bowl for me.

'Right, Alfie, that was quite a morning and I really feel so glad that Aleksy is happy at school again thanks to you.' She made a drink and sat at the breakfast bar in the kitchen. I jumped up onto one of the high stools to be next to her. 'And we've loved having you here. I do miss you,' she said, stroking the part of my neck that I loved. I purred melodiously. 'But you can come here anytime, you know. I know we have competition with Claire and Polly, but you will always have a home with us too.' As she smiled and sipped her drink, she had a dreamy look in her eyes. I tilted my head towards her, questioningly. She smiled, as if she was far away. 'When I first met you, well we had just moved from Poland and I was terrified.'

I miaowed to tell her that I was in the same boat.

'I remember seeing you and you were such a sweet cat; we loved you from the start. And now, we've all had our ups and downs – we even nearly lost you! – but life is good at last. I have a nice home, my husband is successful and my boys are doing well. When we lived in Poland and were struggling to find work, I honestly never thought that we would be in such a good place. You've always been part of that for us.' I miaowed again. I felt the same.

'Right, well I need to clean my nice home. Do you want to keep me company?' She got off the stool and I jumped down. I did want to keep her company and although she barely spoke for the next few hours until she had to leave to get the children from school, I felt close to her, my companion, a lovely woman who was so strong and I was so pleased to see that life had paid off for her. Actually it had paid off for both of us.

-CHAPTER-
Twenty

By the time I got back to Claire's, was fussed over by her and Jonathan, and had something to eat I felt it was quite late. Claire had picked me up that evening, and I had been pleased to see her but also a little bit sad at leaving Franceska and the family. Especially Aleksy. It made me feel sad, and I wished that they lived back on Edgar Road.

But I wanted to find Tiger; I had only been away a few days but I had missed her. I wanted to hear the street gossip as well of course.

Jonathan and Claire had clearly had a lovely time; they were both smiling and looking relaxed, so when they went to the living room to 'chill out' after we'd all eaten, I decided to go out.

Tiger was in her back garden, staring at the moon which had just appeared in the darkening sky. She looked like a picture, sitting up regally, neck long and tail curled about her. I felt a pang of tenderness as I observed her; I had missed my friend.

'Tiger,' I said, softly, as I approached.

'Hey, Alfie, you're back.' She smiled and blinked in greeting.

'I feel like I've been away for ages,' I explained.

'I know, it was weird not seeing you. But come on, let's go for a stroll and I'll fill you in on what happened when you were away.'

'OK, lead the way.' We walked along in silence. I didn't want to push; conscious of how much I could upset her if I mentioned Snowball.

'There was a bit of drama,' Tiger said, eventually as we made our way down the street. I have to admit to feeling comfort from being on such familiar territory – I'd had a nice time away, but it was good to be home.

'Really? What?' I asked.

'Well, I saw Snowball and she ran off as soon as she saw me, back to her house. She's either very nervous, skittish or rude, or maybe all three.'

'I think she's trying to hide from something,' I offered.

'We know what you think, Alfie,' Tiger sighed. I resolved to tread more carefully.

'Sorry, go on.'

'Well I spoke to Rocky who said that he had caught her having a fight with Tom. Rocky wasn't sure who started it, but something happened and Rocky said he saw blood on her fur. But when he went to her to see if she was all right, she ran off and he couldn't find her.'

'I will kill that Tom. Snowball needs us to be friends with her, see,' I said, forgetting my earlier resolve to avoid talking about her.

'You can't make people be friends with you, Alfie. And I don't exactly know what her problem is but if she's willing to fight Tom I'd say she's one angry cat.' We stopped at a spot where the reflections of the moon and one of the street lights were making patterns on the pavement. We jumped between them, watching the pools of light grow and shrink.

'I'm going to see Tom and tell him to leave her alone anyway,' I said finally. I wouldn't have anyone, not person or cat, being bullied, and I'd had my own problems with Tom when I first moved to Edgar Road so I knew what an aggressive cat he could be.

'I'll come with you to do that, although to be fair he might have been trying to be nice to her. And in other news, Salmon has been flinging his weight around.'

'Oh dear, what's he been doing?'

'Well he says that his family is very close to finding out what the Snells are hiding and even getting them removed from the street.'

'No, surely not!'

'No one really believes him, we think the whole family is just full of hot air. Literally in Salmon's case.' We both snickered.

'But what are we going to do?' I asked.

'We?' Tiger stared at me, I wasn't sure if she was being hostile or not.

'Come on, you're my partner in crime. When I went to Aleksy's school I couldn't have done that without you.'

'Yeah, Alfie, flattery will get you everywhere. Anyway, what are you thinking?'

'I'm still a bit unsure but first of all I want to have a word with Tom and then I think we should confront Salmon.'

'OK, well I can't let you do that on your own – they'll eat you alive. I suppose I'd better come along and help.' Tiger didn't look delighted exactly but she was on side for now. Tomorrow we would take on Tom and Salmon.

After arranging to meet Tiger the following day I went home and found Claire and Jonathan, snuggled up together on the sofa. They were watching a film on the television. I stood in the doorway for a moment to observe them. They really did fit together well and I realized that everything I had been through was worth it for this. It really was. I walked in slowly and jumped up on the sofa, landing on Claire's lap.

'Oh, Alfie,' she said, laughing. 'Did you miss us?'

I miaowed the affirmative. I put my paw on Jonathan's chest so he wouldn't feel left out.

'Well nice to know that, and I'd say we missed you, but we were too busy.' Jonathan winked at Claire as she swatted his arm.

'Jonathan, pipe down!' Claire giggled, turning red.

'Honestly, I don't think Alfie minds even if he understands.' I looked at him, trying to convey that I understood even though I wasn't sure I did.

'I know, but I hope … well, you know what I hope. It was such a fabulous weekend, and I loved every minute. You are the perfect husband, Jon, and I only want your child so badly because I think we will be the perfect family.'

'Darling, I'm not sure that there's such a thing as a perfect family,' Jonathan pointed out.

'Maybe not, but I know it'll be perfect to me.' She snuggled further into her husband and I settled down on both of them, dozing and enjoying the warmth of them, as they finished watching the film.

I was home, but then I always seemed to be home these days, no matter where I was.

CHAPTER

Twenty-One

I woke, feeling refreshed until I remembered that today we had to take on Tom and Salmon.

Claire was humming as she gave me my cat ready meal for breakfast and made coffee and toast for Jonathan. She hummed as she walked upstairs to take her shower and she was *still* humming when she came back downstairs dressed for work.

I watched them both get ready to leave. Jonathan as usual couldn't find his house keys – which were in the bowl by the front door where they were always kept, and Claire hurried him out of the house, still humming happily.

I breathed in the silence of the empty house for a few minutes. I hadn't been alone for a while and, although I loved being around people and fellow cats, it was nice to have a bit of time to myself for once. I thought about the day ahead and resolved that I would seek out Snowball later on. I needed to see her, just to get a glimpse of that beautiful white fur and to speak to her, even if she was horrible to me. I missed her. My heart started beating faster at the thought.

I heard my cat flap bang, which was my doorbell equivalent. I went through to the kitchen and found Tiger sitting on the outside.

'You could have come in,' I said.

'I wasn't sure if the humans had left yet.'

'I don't think they'd mind if you did come in. After all, the first time I came into this house I was uninvited.'

'No, but Jonathan can be a bit grumpy, so I'd rather not risk it.'

'Fair enough.' I rolled on my back for a minute, looking up at the blue sky. The sun was almost coming out and it promised to be a warm day. I hoped that it would also be a good day. After lolling in the warming sun for a few moments we set off.

'Do you know where Tom will be?' I asked, trying, and failing, to feel brave about telling him to lay off Snowball.

'It'll be fine, Alfie, I've got your back,' Tiger said, as if she could read my mind.

Tom lived in a house at the end of the street, but wasn't there much of the time. It was a small house and he lived with a man who wasn't as old as my Margaret had been, but he wasn't far off.

We decided to make our way there as a starting point and I felt braver with Tiger by my side. I'd had numerous run-ins with Tom in the early days of Edgar Road; he was a bit of a loner cat, and he seemed not to like anyone. Apparently he got that from his owner.

It's funny how people say that cats are like their owners – or humans as I prefer to think of them – after all, we all know who the real owners are. For example, Salmon is a busybody, just like his humans. Tom is a loner, just like his. Tiger is a bit like hers; they're homebodies and before she became friends with me she rarely ventured far. And me, well I have so many humans that maybe I am combination of all of them, or perhaps, more accurately, they are a combination of me.

We found Tom licking his paws in his small front yard. It was always a bit overgrown and messy; his human was lucky that he was far enough away from the Goodwins, otherwise they'd be over there leaving notes. Perhaps they already had but he just ignored them.

'Hi, Tom. Are you all right?' I asked in my friendliest voice.

He stopped mid-paw and looked at us.

'It isn't often I get visitors, to what do I owe this pleasure?' When he said 'pleasure' he licked his lips, as if he was about to devour us, but then he softened.

'Look, Tom, we've got no beef with you as you know but some cat told us that you had an altercation with Snowball from number forty-eight and we just wondered what the problem was.'

'So I guess Rocky spilled the beans. He's such an interfering cat.'

'Yes, well he was just concerned actually, as are we,' I said. Tom stood in front of us now on all paws, but his stance wasn't aggressive. I relaxed slightly, making it clear there was no confrontation here.

'All right, if you must know, I was just asking her why she was so rude, and then when she was even ruder to me, things got a bit out of hand.'

'What did you do?' Tiger asked.

'Look she started it. OK, so maybe I shouldn't have stopped her but most of the cats on this street get on all right these days and I just wanted to know why she wouldn't even say hello to me.'

'Go on?' I said.

'She hissed at me, told me to go away and when I laughed at her, she swiped me with her paw. Look, she's scratched my head.' Tom bent his head and we could indeed see a small scratch there.

'But what did you do?' Tiger asked.

'I didn't mean to hurt her but I lost my rag, swiped at her and I caught her a bit with my paw. She was bleeding but I realized what I was doing and stopped, but before I could say

I was sorry, she just ran off.'

I was angry with Tom but also surprised to see he did look contrite.

'You need to stop being aggressive,' Tiger said to Tom, who looked even sorrier.

'I know, Tiger, and I regretted my actions as soon as she ran off. I tried to find her to apologize but she's probably refusing to leave her house.'

'Just leave her alone, OK?' I said and Tom agreed. Although I was angry with him, I could see he was sorry but that didn't fix the problem that now Snowball would be even more solitary than ever.

'OK, one down, one to go,' I stated as we walked away from Tom. 'Although what do you think about what Tom said?' I asked.

'I don't think he meant to hurt her,' Tiger said carefully. 'I think Tom finds it hard to put his old aggressive days behind him sometimes.'

'Let's see what Salmon has to say then.'

'Oh yes, and dealing with Salmon will make Tom look like a … a pussy cat!' She laughed at her own joke. We both slowly made our way in search of Salmon. We passed some of our cat friends on the way, but we didn't invite them along. As Tiger said, it wouldn't do to go in heavy-handed as we wanted information from him, not to annoy or scare him off.

As Tiger and I tried to strategize, I came up with a plan. I could charm most people and actually a fair few cats, but Salmon was more like a hostile dog refusing, steadfastly, to be nice to any of us. Not only was he a busybody but he also thought himself human and above all us cats. That was what made him so tricky to deal with.

'We'll just have to try to kill him with kindness,' I suggested.

'I get the first bit, not the second. Maybe we should have got the others to come with us and we could have pinned him down and made him talk.'

'Tiger, sometimes your aggression takes me by surprise. You sound like Tom!'

She grinned at me, she could be one feisty cat.

We reached Salmon's house and found him sitting staring out of the living room window, with the net curtain hanging behind him.

'So what now?' Tiger asked. I instinctively jumped up onto the windowsill in front of him, only the glass separating us. He looked a bit taken aback as I smiled, charmingly. I raised my paw and gestured to him to come outside. He scowled. I could see his whiskers twirling as he contemplated his next move. After a while he jumped down and disappeared.

'Let's go round the back,' I said to Tiger and I jumped down to rejoin her.

We ran round to the back of the house and waited by the back door.

'He's not coming,' Tiger said, after waiting for what felt like ages, and lying down on the small but immaculate lawn that the Goodwins had. Their garden was very pleasant in fact. They had lots of flowers and attractive bushes, the perfect place for playing and chasing butterflies. It was a shame that Salmon would never let us play here.

Tiger was rolling on the lawn and I was playing with some rather nice leaves that were swaying in the breeze, when we heard the cat flap clank and Salmon finally appeared.

'Hi,' I said, breezily. 'How are you?'

He narrowed his eyes at me, flicked his tail, and bared his teeth.

'What on earth are you two doing here?' he asked. Before I could reply, he continued. 'And don't think that I am at all happy about you jumping up at me like that.'

'Sorry but we were just trying to get your attention. You see, my owners were talking about the meeting they had here the other day, you know about the bad neighbours,' I said. Tiger started to object but I silenced her with a look.

'Bad neighbours?' Salmon gave me another suspicious look. 'Last I heard you were all keen on them, or on that white ball of fluff anyway.'

'No, not at all, well I was to be honest but I heard my owners talking about how they were definitely not good for Edgar Road.' My plan to ingratiate myself with Salmon to get information was underway. I would have made a great spy, I thought.

'Really? Well it's about time the other residents came round to our way of thinking. I know Vic and Heather have been pretty upset by people trying to argue against us.'

'Oh I think you'll find that they'll be with you from now on,' I said. I hoped I didn't sound as insincere as I felt. Tiger had turned her back, she was probably trying not to laugh.

'Well that's good.' He still didn't sound convinced.

'But anyway, I heard that that "white ball of fluff" was horrible to you, so we thought we would come and offer support.'

'Really?'

'Of course,' I said.

'She hissed at me.'

'She hisses at everyone.' That much was true.

'Anyway, I might as well tell you. I told the others, as we're

188

really close to finding out what they're up to. The police have been round again and although they didn't arrest anyone, it's obvious that they're actually a criminal gang, masquerading as a normal family.'

'What?!' I was incredulous. 'That's the most ridiculous thing I have ever—' I saw Salmon's eyes narrow at me suspiciously and I remembered my plan. 'I mean really? It seems incredible but it would make sense,' I quickly corrected myself.

'Vic and Heather saw a film once and it was similar. They live in a middle-class street and pretend to be normal but actually they're criminal masterminds.'

'What criminal activities are they supposed to be doing?' I was sure this was all fantasy but I couldn't help feel intrigued.

'That's what we don't know, but clearly the police are onto them. Although Vic says the police can be really dumb so can't be relied on.'

'So what are you guys going to do?' I asked. Surely this was all ridiculous. The angry beautiful cat, the father who looked worried, the mum who was on the verge of breaking down, the teenage girl who confided her loneliness to me, and the surly boy – none of them seemed likely to be members of the criminal underworld.

'Well, my family think it could be a number of things. It could be something called a white-collar crime, or money laundering, or forgery. They could even be jewel thieves,' Salmon continued, excitedly, hostility forgotten. His eyes were glinting eagerly – after all, being the street's busybody cat, he couldn't resist a good gossip.

'Wow,' I said. 'That's interesting, what are they going to do?'

'Oh don't worry, Alfie, we're onto them and on top of this. We're going to get them removed from the street. They rent the house you know, they don't own it, so it's only a matter of time. And that is what I told Snowball. She'd better get used to being homeless.'

'Really?' I asked, seething inside. 'OK, well you know where we are if you need any help. Isn't that right, Tiger?'

'Huh?' Tiger said. She'd been sunning herself on Salmon's lawn, and was now chasing a butterfly as we interrupted her.

'I said we would help Salmon if he needs us to.'

'Oh, OK?' I realized that Tiger hadn't even been listening. Some bodyguard she was.

We went to play in the park as I wanted to be away from the street, so I could think. As we walked there I relayed the conversation I had just had to Tiger.

'I can't believe you didn't listen,' I moaned.

'I got distracted by the shadows the sun cast on the lawn, it was really fun chasing them.' At least she had the grace to sound contrite.

'So what are you going to do when Salmon actually asks for our help?' Tiger asked, after I'd explained what happened.

'It won't come to that, Tiger. The thing is that now I know what the Goodwins are up to, we know what we're dealing with. Now all I have to do is to find out exactly what's going on with Snowball's family, that's my next step.'

'Great, Alfie.' Tiger shook her head. 'I still don't know why you even care.' We were lounging in a warm flower bed, swatting the odd fly that came our way.

'You know me, I like everyone to be happy, cats and humans alike. It means a lot to me.'

'Are you in love with her?' she asked me seriously.

'I don't know,' I replied, honestly.

'Tell me how she makes you feel?' she asked, suddenly getting onto all fours and looking me in the eye. I knew this was a touchy subject, but I wanted to be honest.

'She's mean to me but I still want to see her all the time. I think about her before I go to sleep and when I wake. My tummy does little flips whenever I catch a glimpse of her, I want to be near her, even if she doesn't want to be near me. That's pretty much it.'

'Well, it definitely sounds like you're in love with her,' Tiger said.

'How can you be so sure?' I asked.

'If you haven't figured that out you're not as clever as you think.'

'Huh?'

'I can be sure, Alfie, because that's how I feel about you.'

I was stunned as Tiger shot me one last glance, before running away, leaving me alone in a flower bed with a fly buzzing around my ears.

-CHAPTER-
Twenty-Two

Well, that piece of information certainly set the cat among the pigeons. If I thought I was going to try to find Snowball after that little bombshell I was sadly mistaken. I know Tiger had been acting a little bit differently towards me lately – well, since Snowball entered the scene – and I'd been warned by others that she had feelings for me, but I valued Tiger so highly as a friend I guess I hadn't wanted to confront any of that. And now I'd been forced to, I had no idea what to do.

My head was reeling and I knew I wasn't nearly sharp enough for the task. In fact, I really needed to have a bit of time to think. And of course I didn't do great thinking on an empty stomach. Although it wasn't yet tea time, I realized that if I caught Polly in the house I might get a snack, which would certainly help my focus.

I let myself in through my cat flap and was delighted to see Polly in the kitchen, cooking. The children were both nearby – Henry sat in his booster seat at the table, drawing, and Martha was in her highchair eating carrots. I miaowed loudly.

'Alfie!' Henry shouted, grinning broadly. I grinned back and blinked at him. Polly petted me and then without speaking she went to the fridge and took out some milk. She poured it into a bowl and then got my special biscuits out of the cupboard and tipped some of them into another bowl. I quite enjoyed the biscuits, they were tastier than they looked and worked well with my milk. As I finished them off, then cleaned myself and my whiskers, my mind returned to the problem of Tiger's declaration.

I curled myself up on the sofa in the living room as Polly put a DVD on the television for Henry. He was soon engrossed in it, whilst across the room Martha was just as engrossed as she practised her standing – she finally seemed to be getting the hang of it. Polly sank onto the sofa and I curled up on her lap. It was so comforting to be there as all manner of strange and confusing thoughts about Tiger raced through my brain.

I knew I'd been warned that she felt romantically towards me but I'd put it to the back of my mind and I certainly hadn't taken it seriously. I might have known but I pushed it away because I didn't want to deal with it. Tiger was my buddy and I didn't want anything to change that. However, feelings were already changing that. The more I thought about it the more I realized that I wasn't sure how I was going to fix this one. It seemed to me that as soon as I thought I had one problem under control, another would present itself.

I wished I could talk to Jonathan, because before he met Claire he had lots of women in his life. Although thinking about it, he generally got rid of them pretty quickly. Nor did they seem to be very happy about it.

I didn't want to get rid of Tiger, I loved having her as my friend, but I didn't want a romantic relationship. I needed to be honest with her about how I felt, but the last thing I wanted to do was to hurt her feelings. Oh, it was such a conundrum! The only thing for it was to sleep. Polly stroked me gently, talking to the children every now and then, and I could hear Henry's laughter and Martha's occasional tears as I drifted off.

★★★

Polly gently moved me, waking me up. I yawned and stretched and then, miaowing my goodbyes, I made my way back to Claire and Jonathan's. The house was empty, so I made my way to my favourite spot in the living room, where the sun streamed through the window. I rolled around in a big patch of sunlight, enjoying the warmth and the feeling of the soft carpet against my fur; it was as nice as sunbathing, but in the comfort of my own home.

A little while later, I heard the key in the door and Claire rushed in, all smiles. I smiled and purred as we greeted each other.

'Hey, Alfie, Jonathan has a work thing so I'm having a girls' night,' she said. I wondered if I would get to see mine and Claire's friend Tasha.

'Yes, Alfie, Tash is coming,' Claire said as if she could read my mind, 'as well as Polly and Franceska.' I purred my approval. My favourite human women all under one roof. It would be a good night, even if I was the only man.

I prepared by eating my tea and cleaning myself thoroughly so I looked my best. I sat in front of the big hall mirror, and slicked my fur down so it wasn't sticking up. I tilted my head to check how I looked from all angles and after a while I was satisfied with my appearance. Claire approached and laughed at me.

'Oh, Alfie, you are a vain little cat,' she said. I bristled. I was certainly not vain, I just liked to make sure I looked my best at all times like any self-respecting cat. Still reeling from the accusation, I followed Claire into the kitchen where she took wine glasses out of the cupboard and put some plated nibbles on the table. She still had that glow from Paris about her and she was still singing to herself as she got ready to receive her friends.

Franceska arrived first with a bottle tucked under her arm,

so I prepared for my first lot of fussing. Tasha followed soon after, with such an enormous bunch of flowers that I could barely see her. As Claire greeted her and then ushered her into the kitchen to join Franceska, I could see her baby bump was beginning to show. I remembered Polly's when she was pregnant with Martha; I thought she looked a bit like an egg to be honest but I understood now that when babies grew inside you they made you fat – cats and humans alike. I was quite grateful that it was a female thing.

I curled up on Tasha's lap as they sat around the kitchen table. I knew this wouldn't exactly thrill Claire – she didn't like me being to near human food, but I took a chance and luckily she didn't say anything. Claire and Franceska sipped wine and Tasha sipped a soft drink. They were commenting on the fact that Polly still hadn't arrived, and how it wasn't like her to be late.

'I'll text her. Maybe the kids aren't settling tonight?' Franceska suggested. As she did that, Claire turned her attention to Tasha.

'Are you finding work easier?' she asked. When I first moved here Claire and Tasha worked together, but not anymore and I knew Claire missed her still.

'Yes, but I wish I was back at the old place. Here they want a pound of flesh, pregnant or not. To be honest I think they're a bit annoyed that I'm pregnant; after all I've only been there a year and it was a promotion,' Tasha replied.

'Are they that bad?' Franceska asked, rejoining the conversation.

'Probably not, I think I'm a bit oversensitive. It's just that there's a lot going on and I'm not feeling the sympathy I want,' she said with a wry smile. They all laughed.

'You mean they aren't treating you as a delicate little flower?' Claire teased.

'Exactly.'

The doorbell interrupted them and Claire jumped up. I waited with Tasha, being particularly comfortable, but I was as surprised as everyone else when Claire walked in with not just Polly but Karen Snell behind her.

'Everyone, this is Karen,' Polly introduced. 'Karen, this is Claire, Franceska and Tasha.'

'Hello.' Tasha looked at her with interest as did I.

'Hi.' She looked awkward, as if she was going to turn and run away again.

'Pull up a pew, Karen. Karen recently moved next door to us,' Claire explained as Karen reluctantly took a seat. I had never seen anyone look less pleased to be there and it seemed that no one knew what to say exactly. Claire put two glasses of wine in front of Karen and Polly.

'Thanks, lovely,' Polly said.

'So how do you like Edgar Road?' Tasha asked innocently. Karen looked at her as if she was an alien.

'Karen is having a bit of a time of it with some of the neighbours,' Polly interjected. At the sound of that, Karen burst into tears.

'Oh no, don't cry!' Claire exclaimed. Franceska pulled her chair next to Karen's and put her arm around her.

'I picked Karen up outside as she was being accosted by the Goodwins. Someone had to help her escape that terrible pair!' Polly explained. The atmosphere had changed and it suddenly felt oppressive.

'Street busybodies,' Claire explained to Tasha.

'Anyway,' Polly continued, 'they were threatening to call

the landlord, unless Karen told them why the police were there the other day – it was all very silly but upsetting at the same time as you might imagine.'

'The police?' Franceska asked, wide-eyed.

'Never mind that.' Polly shot her a look. 'Anyway, I'm afraid I've made enemies of the Goodwins now.'

'We need some help though,' Karen mumbled through her tears. She was brandishing some pieces of paper but I couldn't see what was on them.

'Why, what's going on?' Claire asked, full of concern. I pricked up my ears.

'It's our cat, Snowball. She's gone missing.' She held up a poster and I found myself looking at the love of my life. Well her picture anyway.

-CHAPTER-
Twenty-Three

As the women mobilized to help Karen look for Snowball – who'd been missing since the fight with Tom and Salmon – I needed to see Tiger, but I was scared. I knew we still needed to have 'the talk', cat to cat, but now Snowball might be in danger, my priorities had shifted. I was so afraid of many things, but losing Tiger's friendship, and losing Snowball scared me equally.

I know that men aren't known for being good at these things, but I vowed to do what all men and women should do when it came to such delicate matters. Instead of lying or pulling out meaningless platitudes I was going to tell the truth and speak from the heart. Because I needed her more than ever now.

I risked meeting her family as I jumped through the cat flap, and Tiger seemed to appear almost immediately. I could hear voices from another room so I guessed I was in the clear.

'Hey, what are you doing here?' she asked.

'Look, I know we need to talk, but I've just seen Karen Snell. She was in tears because Snowball is missing. She hasn't been home since the altercations with Tom and Salmon.' I sounded hysterical, I know, but I felt it too. I was so afraid for Snowball, and I understood why Karen was so inconsolable.

'Alfie, do you think she might have been hurt more badly than Tom and Salmon led us to believe?'

'But even Rocky said she ran off. She can't have been hurt too badly if she could still run surely?'

'OK, come on, we'll round up the others and start a search

party. Don't worry, Alfie, we'll find her.' Tiger gave me a reassuring look and I knew I'd never have a better friend.

'About earlier,' I said as we walked towards Nellie's house to get her first. Tiger was being really sweet over the missing Snowball but what if she didn't want to ever be my friend again? I tried to tell myself not to be so dramatic, but a cat can't change its fur.

'Alfie, it's OK. I know you don't have *those* feelings for me,' Tiger said.

'You do?' I was taken aback.

'I'm not stupid, Alfie. I've known you for three years; you meet white fluff-ball for a second and you're in love. Don't worry, I know that we're just friends, and I know that deep down you respect my feelings but like a man, sometimes you can be a bit insensitive to them.'

'Wow,' I managed to say. Now I know why my human males said women were so much better at this stuff. It was like she could read my mind. I continued, 'I wanted to tell you honestly how I felt. I love you, Tiger, but as a friend, and as a friend I couldn't love you more. You're right, it's different with Snowball. I don't know why, but that's how it is.'

'I know, Alfie. If you felt the same way about me it would be so easy, but you don't and we need to move on.'

'And I thought this conversation was going to be tricky,' I said feeling bemused. I was confused again but in a different way. A good way.

'I don't want to lose you from my life, Alfie, and that means I have to accept that we are just friends and stop being so jealous of Fluff-ball.' She looked at me but she was smiling. I purred and nuzzled.

'You are so amazing, Tiger, the best friend a cat could have.'

'You always say that.'

'Because it's true. Are you sure you're OK with this?' I was still concerned.

'I will be. Alfie, I want things to go back to the way they were with us before, and if that means I have to hear about Fuzzy-kitten and her weird family then so be it.' Tiger smiled to show me the name-calling was in good humour.

'Thank you so much Tiger, you mean the world to me.' I meant it.

'Right, well come on, let's find Snowball, and make sure she's all right.'

We found Nellie at the end of the street, watching the moon. While she went to find Rocky and Elvis, we started our hunt but then we bumped into Tom.

'Tom, are you sure you didn't hurt Snowball more than you said?' I asked, angrily. I was worried now and upset, and although Tiger was being amazing I hated to think of Snowball out there, scared and hurt.

'Honestly it was nothing major. She could still walk away. Why are we raking this up again, I said I was sorry.' He looked a bit sheepish as Tiger stepped forward.

'She's gone missing,' Tiger explained. 'Her owner has Alfie's families out looking for her now, but she hasn't been home since she fought with you and argued with Salmon.'

'I didn't mean for anything bad to happen.' Tom did look stricken, I had to admit. 'I'll do whatever it takes to help you find her.'

'You're the last person she'd want to see,' I pointed out, 'please don't look for her. You might scare her off again.'

'OK, but I really do want to help you.'

'Maybe go and see what you can find out from other cats. If you hear anything, come and find one of us,' Tiger said and we bounded off.

We both searched well into the night, as far as the park at one end of the road, while the other cats covered the other end.

'No sightings could mean that she isn't too injured to hide,' Tiger said.

'But she's probably hungry and scared. Do you think that maybe Salmon saying that the family were going to be hounded out, tipped her over the edge?'

'Probably, I know she's having a hard time settling in. She could have gone back to her old home,' Tiger suggested.

'I guess we need to go home and get some rest now. We can't stay out forever.' I was tired, cold and losing hope. I needed to regain my strength and think logically about where she could be. It was important that I had a strategy and, so far, there were no leads and I could no longer think straight. Every lamp-post we passed on our way home now had pictures of Snowball on them; her beautiful face was everywhere. I had never known worry like this but I gave up and went to get some rest. Although I knew I wouldn't properly rest until I'd found her, I curled up into my bed.

-CHAPTER-
Twenty-Four

I slept uneasily which wasn't a surprise. I made my way downstairs where Claire and Jonathan were already sat at the breakfast table.

'Polly texted me to say she'd called in at the Snells' and there was still no sign.'

'God, I remember how worried I was when Alfie was missing, when he'd been hurt and taken to the vet's that time.' I shuddered as I made my presence felt. I hated hearing that word.

'Oh there you are, I wonder if you've seen Snowball?' He went to feed me. I miaowed to tell him I hadn't seen her.

'They're making more posters. Polly said she would take the kids out and put them up a bit further afield. I can't get out of work but I've offered for us both to help when we get back.'

'OK, darling, cool. I'll try not to be late.'

After I'd breakfasted, groomed myself and made my way out, I saw Polly and Karen and I wanted to cry as I saw Snowball's beautiful face smiling down at me again and wondered if I would ever see her again. You heard about cats going missing a lot and many of them were never found. Terrible things could happen, and it was unfortunately more common than it should be. I felt as if my heart was going to break. It seemed Karen felt the same because she stood with Polly, sobbing as Polly put her arm around her and the children looked on.

'I'm sorry,' Karen said. 'But she's family. Daisy adores her and we've had her since she was a kitten. I can't bear to lose her after everything else we've lost.'

'Hey, love, come on, we'll find her. After work me, Matt,

Claire and Jonathan are going to look. We've put these posters up everywhere and I'm sure we'll have her home safe in no time.' I hoped that Polly was more confident than she sounded.

I left them, as Tim joined his wife and for the first time I saw affection pass between them. They clung to each other and when Tim suggested driving around looking for Snowball, Karen said she wanted to go with him.

I had to find that cat. As I started walking I saw Tiger engaged in some kind of conversation with Salmon. I quickened my pace. Maybe he would know where Snowball was.

'Hi, Tiger,' I said.

'Ah, here's your partner. I've just discovered your ruse, Alfie,' Salmon said unkindly.

'What?' I asked.

'Sorry, Alfie, I felt I had to tell him we were just pretending to be on his side the other day, as we're doing all we can to find Snowball.'

'Oh, I'd forgotten that.'

'Well who cares. The cat is done for.'

'What do you mean?' I hissed angrily.

'It's obvious. She's been kidnapped by the criminals that the Snells are involved with. They've probably double-crossed them or something and so they've taken the cat.'

'I've never heard such nonsense,' Tiger said.

'We'll see,' Salmon replied before stalking off.

'Ignore him, Alfie, I'm sure she'll be all right,' Tiger said, trying to cheer me up. I smiled, gratefully, at her but even I was losing hope as no one had seen her. We had looked everywhere we could think of and were quickly running out of ideas.

★★★

That evening, I felt the love in Edgar Road, for the first time in ages, as Polly, Matt, Claire and Jonathan and all the Snells came out together to look for Snowball. I had cat tears in my eyes as I saw them all working together. I had wanted to bring them together, to help them, but not at the expense of Snowball. As her face looked at me from every lamp-post I tried to strengthen my resolve to find her but even I was struggling to stay positive.

'I just can't think of where else to look,' Tim said as they all converged outside our house. My families exchanged anxious glances.

'But, Dad, we can't give up,' Daisy said, tears streaming. Her father put his arm around her.

'We'll never give up, princess.' He hugged her.

'Hey, I know,' Matt said, trying to sound optimistic. 'Why don't we try another search but this time split up? I know we've looked but she might have got lost and be trying to find her way back. Tim and Christopher, come with me and Jonathan and we'll head east, you ladies go west and we'll meet back at ours where I'll get our babysitter to make us some hot drinks.'

Everyone agreed but I couldn't help but feel that it was because they didn't know what else to do. The only silver lining, I thought glumly, was that at least we were showing the Snells what a nice street we were, with the exception of the Goodwins of course.

'What now?' Tiger asked me. The other cats were all still searching but like the humans, we were running out of places to look. I began to feel despondent but then I remembered who I was.

'Remember when I went to stay at Franceska's?' I asked. Tiger nodded. 'I met this outdoor cat, Dustbin, he works the yard outside big Tomasz's restaurant, keeping it clean from vermin.'

'Nice job,' Tiger said. 'But I don't follow.'

'He's an expert on being outside. I know it's a bit further but maybe he can help us find Snowball!' I just had a feeling that he would be better at this than we were.

'Alfie, it's getting dark and it's quite far away. Are you sure about this?' Tiger asked. She was right, this was out of my comfort zone, and I didn't relish the idea.

'I have to find Snowball and this is the only idea I've got,' I explained.

'You must really love her,' Tiger said, sounding a bit sad.

'I'd do the same for you,' I replied and I meant it. I loved her in a different way but I would.

'I know, come on, let's find this Dustbin.'

We walked as briskly as we could, with an urgency that we didn't feel the last time we came here, and also with more confidence. We both knew we could find our way back easily. The only difficult part was when we got to the restaurant finding our way out the back, after all I had only been through the flat before. But we found an alley and after a couple of wrong turns we found the yard.

'Dustbin,' I called. A head emerged from under a bin. He had clearly been having his dinner.

'Alfie? Is that you?' He crawled out.

'Hi, yes, and this is my friend Tiger. Dustbin, we really need your help.' I noticed Tiger looking a bit scared as I filled him in. She was a brave cat but she had never had to rough it like this in her life. Not like me. Or Dustbin.

I realized quickly that I had done exactly the right thing as Dustbin seemed to round up quite a few dirty, feral cats who looked terrifying but were all incredibly kind and willing to help. I described Snowball to them – cats don't need missing posters I can tell you – and I even managed to explain how she smelt, although Tiger said I went too far when I went on about garden roses, fresh dew on grass, and summer breezes. You can't help being in love I tried to tell her as the other cats laughed at us. Tiger then shot out a more practical description, also saying that Snowball might not be overjoyed or even remotely friendly if found. She made a good point.

Dustbin said we had to wait for them in the yard, which horrified Tiger; and when they left, I could see she was more nervous than I was.

'What was that?' she said, jumping.

'Your shadow.' I rolled my eyes and flicked my tail. I had been homeless of course, for a short time, and although I hated to be reminded of those days, I knew this yard and it didn't scare me. I was glad the mice and rats were keeping away from us though as we settled down to wait.

I was fighting sleep, but Tiger's jitters kept me awake. She was tougher than me normally but I had found her Achilles paw. It was dawn by the time Dustbin returned with one of his friends and by some miracle they had Snowball with them. At first I wondered if I was so exhausted I was seeing things but as they approached, I saw it was definitely her and I wanted to leap for joy.

'You did right coming to get me,' Dustbin said. I looked at Snowball, who didn't look well. She was thin, as if she hadn't eaten for the whole time she'd been missing – coming up to

213

four days – and she wasn't very white anymore. But still the sight of her made my heart beat that bit faster, although I was also full of anxiety at the state she was in. Would she be all right?

'Dustbin … how?' I was almost lost for words.

'Word got out very quickly, and she was found about two miles north of Edgar Road. She'd got lost, and was hiding out in a park, but near a big estate, so it was fraught with danger. It was lucky one of my mates remembered seeing her and found her when he did, he called me and we managed to get her back to you.' Dustbin looked proud and I went over and thanked him by nuzzling him, although he was filthy.

'Dustbin, I don't know how to thank you,' I said.

'No worries, Alfie, happy to help. But she doesn't look too good. How are you going to get her back to Edgar Road?'

'I'm not sure.' I couldn't quite believe they'd found her so quickly, I certainly hadn't got a clue how to get her home. She didn't look as if she would be able to walk.

'Franceska and Tomasz?' I said. It was almost morning, but I would have to wait until they got up. 'But how can I get their attention?' I said.

'Ah, well, you might be in luck. Franceska comes down here every morning to clean the restaurant, she does it before the boys get up.'

'Thank goodness.' I was relieved, and Tiger looked as if she could finally relax.

'And until then, we need to all snuggle up to keep warm.'

Tiger looked horrified at the idea but she moved close to me. Snowball still hadn't spoken and she looked as if she was in shock as she lay down next to Dustbin, I snuggled up to her other side, so she would be warm between us, and because I wanted to be close to her as the relief of finding her was seeping in. I hoped she wasn't too ill, but I couldn't be sure, as we all fell into an uneasy sleep.

'What on earth?' I heard Franceska shout, which woke us with a start. She ran back upstairs and came down again with big Tomasz, who was wearing his pyjamas.

'Alfie?' he said.

'Yes is Alfie, but with the cat who went missing and this cat from his street also.' Franceska obviously recognized Tiger. 'And Dustbin. What is going on?' We all miaowed in chorus, apart from Snowball who was still silent.

'The cat looks sick.' Tomasz picked Snowball up and she lifted her head and looked at him, which gave us all hope.

'But what are they doing here?' Franceska asked.

'No idea, but we need to get them home. You stay with the boys, I'll get dressed and then drive them back.'

'But we don't have cat carriers.'

'*Kochanie,* we don't have time to worry about that.'

Tomasz placed us in the car, all on the back seat. Snowball had managed to say thank you to Dustbin before we left and then she said the same to me and Tiger. It was the sweetest sound ever to my ears, like flapping butterfly wings. I tried to enjoy the journey but I was too full of emotion. We had done it, or Dustbin had; my plan had worked out. It was amazing and I couldn't wait to get home, so that Snowball could get better. I had a horrid feeling that she was going to have to visit the vet though.

Tomasz pulled up outside Jonathan and Claire's house, and rang the bell. He was carrying Snowball and I was at his feet. Tiger bade us goodbye and went home to eat, sleep and get clean, something I was also desperate to do. Finally Jonathan appeared, looking grumpy and wearing his dressing gown.

'What on earth are you doing here, Tomasz?' he asked before he saw that Snowball was in his arms. 'You found Snowball? How on earth?' He looked at me.

'I have no idea, Jonathan. I found Alfie, with the missing cat, in the yard behind the restaurant, along with the restaurant cat.'

'I don't understand,' Jonathan said.

'I don't either,' Tomasz concurred. 'It seems that Alfie strikes again.'

Claire appeared and took in the scene. 'What's going on?'

'He's got Snowball! It seems that, yet again, Alfie is somehow linked to a success story and we will never know what happened.' Jonathan stood aside as if to let Tomasz in.

'She is not good, I think we need to get her home now,' Tomasz said, staying on the doorstep.

'Oh, I'll come round with you,' Jonathan offered.

The Snells cried tears of joy when they saw Snowball, but the celebration was short-lived as they noticed how unwell she seemed.

'Do you need a lift to the vet?' Tomasz asked, introducing himself.

'No, we can't thank you enough for bringing her back but we'll take it from here.' As the Snells shut the door, Jonathan and Tomasz exchanged a glance; it seemed as if the Snells were keen to get rid of them and me.

'They seem a bit strange,' Tomasz said. 'They didn't even ask me where the cat was found or anything.'

'I know, and I thought we all bonded yesterday when we were looking for her. I mean they didn't tell us their life story but they joined us for tea and cake, and although they were upset they were friendly then.'

Both men shrugged and I wondered what this meant. Would the Snells return to their old ways or were they going to continue being part of the street? I fervently hoped it was the former but I was afraid it was the latter.

CHAPTER

Twenty-Five

I was more determined than ever to come up with a plan to help Snowball and her family. As I feared, the Snells had retreated to their old ways since Snowball's return a few days ago. They had come to see Jonathan to tell him that Snowball was fine; she had been just a bit dehydrated. The vet had given her some medicine and the all clear, and they had thanked us, and finally even asked where she was found. That was the last we'd seen of them.

Desperate to see Snowball, I had taken to hanging out by the loose fence panel and I had been rewarded with her finding me there three days after her rescue.

'Are you all right?' I asked her.

'I am now, thank you. And thank you for your efforts to find me.' She sounded formal for someone whose life I'd practically saved.

'We all did. The cats on Edgar Road and my friend Dustbin all rallied. Even Tom who is sorry he hurt you. But why did you run off?' I asked.

'I'd had enough. My family were falling apart, Tom and Salmon were mean and I thought if I was going to be homeless anyway I might as well make a head start. By the time I'd cooled off and wanted to come home I had no idea where I was until that cat found me.'

'I remember how scary it can be out on the streets,' I said.

'Well thank you again, Alfie, and you might be pleased to know my family are stronger now. While I was missing, they remembered how much they loved each other, so they are

221

getting along much better. At least one good thing came out of it.'

'I'm so glad; now if only we could all be friends—'

'Don't get ahead of yourself. We still need our privacy, they still have too much going on to cope with and, speaking of that, I'm afraid Tim is fixing the fence today. When he saw how loose this panel was, which I may have helped him discover, he decided to do some work out here. Thanks for finding me, but now you can leave us alone again.'

That was over a week ago and I hadn't even so much as caught a glimpse of Snowball since. The loose fence panel had been fixed, and so my days of looking from my garden into the Snells' were over. After all I'd done for her, I was hurt. But then I realized I couldn't give up.

I decided it was time to go and see Snowball to find out once and for all what was going on with her family. I had to try to get to the bottom of it. I was prepared to be brave and go inside the house if I needed to; after all, I knew the layout and this time I would make sure I avoided getting stuck in cupboards.

I was still feeling quite pleased with myself as I made my way next door, going over the fence rather than round the front. I surveyed the place from the top of the fence, but couldn't see anything, so I jumped down into the garden. It was deserted, I could tell by just sniffing the air. I went over to look through the patio doors. Whilst the Snells kept the front of the house in darkness most of the time, I could see into the back, and as I looked through the patio doors, trying not to concentrate too much on my own reflection, I could see the kitchen was empty. I decided to take my chance as I hopped through the cat flap. The kitchen was definitely empty, not tidy though, as dishes littered the side and there was a lot of clearing up to be done. Being such a clean cat this made me bristle but I tried not to mind too much. Snowball's bowls on the floor had half-eaten food and a small amount of water. As tempted as I was to help myself, I didn't touch them as I knew that would definitely upset her. And of course I was glad she was well enough to eat again.

I padded through the hall and into the living room, which was much like ours at home, although, again, not as tidy. Evidence of life could be seen in the creases on the cushions, and I spied some bits of white fur on the sofa. I couldn't resist having a sniff, making me feel closer to the object of my affections. As always, the front curtains were drawn. I reluctantly went back into the hallway and stood at the bottom of the staircase. I was so tempted to go upstairs, to see what was there, but then I heard movement coming from the kitchen. I froze. Was I about to be discovered? I looked for somewhere to hide but there was nowhere, and so I stood rooted to the spot as a figure appeared. It was Christopher, the boy that they talked about. He started as he saw me and then smiled.

'Snowball won't be happy to find another cat in the house,' he said. 'Unless of course you're her friend? Do cats have friends?' He bent down to stroke me and read my collar. 'Oh you're the cat who helped find her. Nice one.'

I miaowed, trying to answer him, but he didn't seem to hear me. He threw a backpack on the floor and went into the living room. As he slumped on the sofa, I wondered what I should do. I mean here was an opportunity for me to get a bit more information, but I also didn't know what Snowball would say if she came home and found me talking to another of her humans. But the temptation was too great and, yet again, trying not to think too much about consequences, I hopped up on the sofa and sat with Christopher.

'I shouldn't be here,' he said, looking at me, darkness clouded his eyes. 'I should be in school. There's going to be loads of crap when Mum and Dad find out, and we're all getting on better so I don't want to hurt them anymore.' He sounded sad and a bit angry. 'Luckily they're both out. Mum at work as always and Dad's out trying to find a new job, and isn't having much luck. It's all so bad here no wonder Snowball ran away.' I purred my agreement, although I didn't exactly understand.

'That's the thing,' he continued. 'I have no one to talk to. My old friends all managed to forget me instantly, and I hate my new school. Daisy is so self-obsessed she barely notices I'm here, same with the parents, and even the cat doesn't want to listen to me – Snowball is Daisy's cat so she doesn't pay much attention to me.'

I miaowed again, to tell him I at least wanted to listen.

'I understand now why my parents are so damn paranoid after everything that happened. People suck. My mates on Facebook ignore me, or post that my dad is a criminal, which isn't true. They post up pictures of parties I'm not invited to, holidays we can't afford to go on and, well, when I message them they never reply.'

I had no idea what this Facebook was but I got the gist. He had lost his friends when he moved, just like I had. I nuzzled him. Life was hard when you felt alone and I knew all about that.

'Although when Snowball was missing the neighbours who helped seemed nice but now, Mum and Dad have gone back to ignoring everyone.' He sighed. I purred to try to say I wished they would be friends with everyone.

'If only he hadn't done that to Dad. We have to put up with the police coming round, although I know they are trying to help but it doesn't help when the neighbours are gossiping about us. None of this was our fault. None of it was Dad's fault although I don't tell him that enough.'

I held my breath; who did 'he' mean and what had he done? Was I finally going to find out what had happened to the Snells. A loud and unhappy noise interrupted us. I turned and looked; Snowball was sitting in front of the sofa and she was not happy. I didn't hear her come in so had no idea how much of that she had heard. She hissed at me and Christopher laughed. I was so happy to see her that I didn't care about her anger, and I was also pleased to see she looked back to her normal beautiful self.

'For God's sake, Snowball! Alfie rescued you.' Snowball hissed again. I didn't know what to do as I looked from Christopher to my one true love. I was still enamoured with her but her timing sucked – I had to admit – just as I was getting to the bottom of things.

'All right, keep your fur on,' he said at last, as he picked me up. 'Sorry, Alfie, looks like you're going to have to leave. Apparently there's only room for one cat in this house.' He smiled at me as he opened the front door and gently set me down outside. My last view before the door closed on me was of Snowball's thunderous face as she glared at me.

Well, that didn't go exactly to plan.

When I got home, I crawled into my bed. Life was complex for humans and cats alike, although I was quickly realizing that it was relationships that caused most complexities in life. I thought about it, how others affect you, the impact they have on your life, both good and bad. I knew that my skill was bringing people together and I was determined that, despite resistance, I would continue to do this. Relationships were worth it in the long run even if they caused heartache along the way, I thought as I drifted off into an uneasy sleep.

-CHAPTER-

Twenty-Six

'Why do I have to do everything?' Claire's shrill voice shattered my sleep. I stood up, stretched, and shook the sleep off me, before I ventured downstairs. Claire rarely shouted and I was unused to it. I found her and Jonathan in the kitchen; she looked incensed and he looked slightly scared.

'I'm sorry, but I didn't know you wanted me to go to the supermarket on my way home from work.'

'Because you never bloody ask! You just expect food to magically appear in the house, despite knowing that I work hard too. I might not earn as much as you but I still contribute to this household,' Claire thundered.

'Darling, I know, and I would never suggest otherwise. Listen, give me a list and I'll go shopping right now.' Jonathan looked startled, like a cat caught in the headlights.

'Yes, of course you'll go now when I've had to shout and scream at you. Forget it, get your own dinner. I'm going for a walk.' The front door shook as Claire slammed it. Jonathan looked at me.

'No idea what's got into her, mate, but I'm not keen.' I miaowed. I wasn't keen either, this was not like my Claire, who never shouted. I was unsure if I should be worried but I was pretty sure I should be.

While Claire stormed off, Jonathan fed me, before sitting at the table and scratching his head a bit more. After an hour Claire returned and he apologized, although I was pretty sure he had no idea what he was actually sorry for. He poured her a glass of wine and after they talked things through, they made up and she eventually forgave him. It was all so strange.

Meanwhile, while they went to bed quite happy, I went to bed worrying about Snowball. I wasn't sure why she was so angry with me. I had helped save her, and then gone to see if she was all right, yet I was being made to feel as if I was in the wrong. It was as if she would never forgive me, not for all the saucers of milk in Edgar Road, although I was only trying to be caring. It was so confusing.

After a fretful sleep I decided that I would take a leaf out of Jonathan's book and apologize even though I hadn't technically done anything bad. I thought about taking Snowball a gift but I didn't want to overdo it. It was easy for me to get a mouse or bird for her – or more accurately, to ask Tiger to get me one as she was the better hunter – but what I needed to do was issue a heartfelt apology to her and hope that she would forgive me. I was pretty sure she wasn't as easy to get round as Claire though; Claire was a lovely pushover when it came to me or Jonathan, but Snowball clearly wasn't that easy to impress.

Decision made, I didn't want to dilly-dally. I ate my breakfast quickly, but took some time cleaning myself, determined to look my best. I quickly made my way to the Snells' back garden next door and hid behind a bush. I sat and waited, as I watched the kitchen scene unfold. It was familiar in a way.

Tim was dishing out breakfast. Daisy was looking at her phone as she ate toast. Christopher looked even more unhappy than he did the previous day, and Karen was drinking a cup of coffee. No one seemed to be speaking. I caught a glimpse of Snowball at her bowl, eating her breakfast, looking happier than when I last saw her, and I bided my time.

Finally, Tim cleared the dishes, Karen left the room and Daisy and Christopher followed shortly after. I guessed they were going to school. Tim loaded the dishwasher and Snowball came outside.

I slid out from my hiding place.

'*You!*' she exclaimed.

'Listen, I've come to apologize. I'm sorry that I was in your house yesterday but I'd only come to find you, to check you were all right. I didn't expect Christopher to talk to me.'

'What did he say?' Her eyes were narrowed.

'Just that someone did something to his dad, someone who he thought was a friend. He didn't say what.'

'Good. That is more than you need to know.' Her tail twitched from side to side angrily.

'Snowball, there is something going on, and I know it's something bad and sometimes it helps to share. I've solved my fair share of problems in my time, both for cats and for humans, and I'm not bad at it, if I do say so myself.'

'Even you can't fix this,' she said.

'But I could try,' I pushed.

'What is it with you? Why won't you just leave us well alone? We don't need you or your help.'

'OK, fine. But can I ask you one thing? Snowball, if I tell you my story, how I came to live next door, and the people in my life then will you agree to listen? And after that if you want me to leave you alone then I will.'

She narrowed her eyes at me again. They really were like glittering sapphires.

'So if I listen to your life story you'll go away?'

'If you want me to.'

'Oh, I'm pretty sure I will. But do carry on. And I'll try not to fall asleep.'

This was one tough cat to win over, but then I loved a challenge.

'You see I am a doorstep cat. Before you moved in I was considering adding the new family here to my list of families I stay with, but of course they already had you.' I tried to sound my most charming as I told her the story. Of my first owner Margaret, of being homeless, of the cats who helped me on my way, and those who tried to hurt me. I told her of reaching Edgar Road, my journey, how I met my families, helped them and brought people together. I left out no detail as I filled her in on my story.

'So you see, I am actually a fairly resourceful cat,' I said.

'Is everything you've told me true?' she asked.

'Absolutely. I do not tell lies.' I was slightly affronted, although I realized I had told her a lot of stories in one go. I sat upright, my tail curled around my body, trying to work out what she thought of it all.

'Well it's quite an adventure. And yes you have obviously proved yourself very helpful to those people but I don't see how that applies to us.'

'Can't you see that if I know what's wrong for your family I can help you guys too?'

'No, you can't.'

'How do you know?'

'I just know. Alfie, listen to me. I'm sure you are a very nice cat. Perhaps in other circumstances we could have been friends even. But now, this is not the time. My family is literally falling apart. They are only together now because of misery and the misery isn't going anywhere. Just as I think things will get better, they get worse again. It's all horrible and we are all tormented. I think that if there was something to be done I would have done it by now.'

'Yes but if I knew … I might have a new perspective.'

'Your life has been amazing, you're right, but it's nothing like mine. And you might have helped others but you can't help us.'

'But I'm sure I can.' I was confident.

'Alfie, you said that all I had to do was to listen to your story.'

'I did,' I admitted.

'And if I still wanted you to keep away you would?'

'I said that too.'

'Well I want you to keep away. From me, from my family and especially from Christopher.'

'But do you really?' I asked, clinging on to my fast-evaporating hope.

'I absolutely do. Goodbye.' She was beating her tail from side to side, and as I looked at her I knew I'd failed.

She disappeared back into her house, her white fur gleaming in the sunlight, and I realized that for once I had overestimated my abilities. I made my way home, slowly, bereft at the idea that I had failed and might never be friends with her, and terrified at the thought that I would only be able to see her from afar and never hear her voice again. I was flooded with disappointment that her family wouldn't be part of our lives, and I felt like a failure as a doorstep cat. A failure at everything. I felt the weight of the world settle on me as I made my way home.

CHAPTER

Twenty-Seven

'I'm worried about Alfie,' I heard Claire say but I didn't lift my head up.

'Why?' Jonathan asked. 'He looks all right to me.'

'You never notice anything,' Claire snapped. She was still in a bit of a mood it seemed. 'He's barely eaten the last few days. I even had to throw away salmon yesterday.'

'Really?' Jonathan started to pay attention.

'Yes, really. Do you think he's ill? He's been in his bed much more than usual and has hardly been out. Or he stares out of the window if he's not in bed. I'm really worried, Jon.'

They should be worried. There was definitely something going on with me. Since Snowball had banished me from her life, I had barely been able to eat and I had no interest in anything, not even seeing Tiger. I had hardly set foot outside the house, and had only done so when I absolutely had to. Tiger had been waiting for me outside my back door, wanting to go and play, and I told her I was feeling unwell, an excuse she reluctantly accepted. The thing was that I actually did feel terrible. I was quite out of sorts. Claire was right, it wasn't like me not to tuck into my food but my appetite was all but gone. I felt like staring into space, had no energy for my usual sports, and all I wanted to do was to curl up in my cat bed, or stare out of the window into nothingness. I didn't feel ill exactly but I certainly didn't feel like myself. And I didn't understand what was wrong with me.

'Shall we take him to the vet?' Jonathan suggested. I wanted to yelp my objection but I didn't even have the energy for that.

'Yeah, if he doesn't perk up by tomorrow I'll take him in. But Jonathan, it's as if he's depressed or something.'

'Do cats get depressed?' Jonathan asked.

'I don't know, but he seems almost like I was when I first moved here. All mopey and lethargic.'

'Blimey, a depressed cat, who'd have thought it. Of course he might just be lovesick.'

'Do you think cats can be lovesick?' Claire asked. Jonathan shrugged and they turned and walked away from me.

But that was it. I was lovesick. Jonathan had hit the nail on the head.

I felt lethargic, sad, and mournful. I knew I was just feeling sorry for myself but being in love, being rejected, does make one a bit self-indulgent, I guess. When Snowball sent me away, I felt as if I'd lost her forever. Not that I ever had her in the first place, but I felt as if I'd lost hope of her ever being mine. And I was the sort of cat that never lost hope.

I pricked up my ears. Claire was still talking about the vet, of which I am definitely not a fan. They prod and poke around where they're not wanted and yes, perhaps they did some good too, but I had them down as people to visit only when necessary. I had far too much on my plate to spend time in the vet's, especially as I now knew that my supposed illness was caused by the lack of love from another cat. No, no way did I want to go to the vet. I quickly realized it was time for me to pull myself together.

I started to process my thoughts. Just because Snowball said she wanted me to stay away didn't mean forever? And the problem with her family hadn't gone away, had it? No, in fact I was needed more than ever, even if she didn't realize it. In fact, if I could help the family, Snowball would surely be so happy that she would definitely want to be my friend at the very least. Although for now I would respect her wishes and stay away, I knew that it wouldn't be forever. Or even very long.

I had begun to regain my resolve but not my appetite; however, I realized that if I was going to prove useful, I needed to keep my strength up. So with all the energy I could muster, I left my bed, approached Claire and miaowed the way I did when I wanted feeding. She looked so happy as she praised me for looking better. Honestly, sometimes it was almost too easy.

I forced myself to eat; it wasn't that I felt sick, I just wasn't that hungry, but after some food and more water, I began to feel a bit stronger. I knew I had to fight the urge to pine, because it was clear that no one ever achieved anything by pining. After four days in bed, it was time to get up.

Next stop was Tiger. After looking in her garden to no avail, I made my way to our recreation space. She was there, with Nellie, Rocky and Elvis. They were sunbathing and passing the time, so I joined them.

'Are you feeling better?' Tiger asked. I nodded.

'What was wrong?' Nellie followed.

'I don't know, I just felt a bit under the weather,' I replied, eager to change the subject. If I was lovesick and pining, the fewer people who knew the better. I had a reputation to maintain after all.

'Guess what, Alfie?' Elvis said.

'What?' I pricked up my ears.

'Tom has a crush on our Tiger,' Rocky quickly piped up.

'Shut up,' Tiger hissed.

'He left her a present, a mouse,' Nellie told me. Tiger just looked at me.

'He's been mooning around after her, and although we

find it quite funny I do feel a bit sorry for him.'

'Hey, enough!' Tiger shouted. 'Tom's a bit rough around the edges but since he's stopped fighting us he's become a nice cat.'

'But what about Snowball?' I said.

'That was his wake-up call, although personally I think it was more Salmon's fault. Alfie, you know he helped us in any way he could when we were looking for Snowball, I think he deserves a second chance.'

I raised my whiskers in question. It seemed maybe Tiger was a little bit keen on Tom if she was willing to give him a 'second chance' and it was true, he had redeemed himself. I was actually delighted for my friend. Being in love, even unre-quited love, made you want everyone else to feel it too.

'Tom's a nice guy now,' I supported my friend. Tiger looked uncomfortable.

'You never used to think that,' Nellie said.

'That was when he tried to bite me all the time but he doesn't do that anymore, and he's said he'll give up fighting,' I replied, magnanimously.

'Glad you think so, Alfie. But anyway, just because he apparently likes me doesn't mean that I feel the same.' Tiger squirmed confirming my instinct was right.

'But do you?' I asked.

'Right, who wants to chase butterflies?' Tiger changed the subject.

Tiger and I went off together, with my promise to help her chase butterflies, although I also had an ulterior motive as we needed to talk.

'Were you really ill?' she asked, as we reached the park and made for the best butterfly bushes.

'No, I was just a bit sad to be honest. I didn't realize it at the time, but that's what it was.'

'Like when humans get depressed?' Tiger asked.

'Yes a bit like that. I didn't want to eat, I was tired, I felt like I had no energy for anything.'

'But now?'

'I'm feeling a bit better. To be honest, I didn't realize that I was so bad, but when my family started talking about the vet I knew I had to do something. So I forced myself to get up and come out.'

'Oh, Alfie, you're not the type of cat to be like that. Is this about Snowball?' She sounded cross, although not jealous.

'I know and that's why it's so infuriating. I know it's a bit awkward but it *is* to do with Snowball. She makes me feel so sad, because she doesn't like me.'

'Right, Alfie, you need a project, because otherwise you might slip back into pining for that incredibly undeserving cat,' Tiger stormed. 'I'd like to give her a piece of my mind.'

'Don't, Tiger, and you're right, I do need a project; if I focus on that then I'll forget about the heart pains I'm feeling.'

'God you're dramatic. But listen, I'll help you. Goodness knows you don't deserve it but I will.' Tiger blinked at me. And I wondered why I couldn't have fallen in love with her. She cared about me so much that life would certainly have been much easier with her; but of course as my humans say 'you don't choose who you fall in love with'. It just happens.

-CHAPTER-
Twenty-Eight

'Alfie, play with the football outside?' Aleksy asked me as he headed out the patio doors. I followed him. It was family day again at our house, and I was almost back to my old self. I was totally myself in front of people – and cats – but I still had the odd moment of pining when I was alone. My heart ached a bit when I pictured Snowball, no matter how fruitless it was; I had no control. But at the same time I was eating again, exercising and on the whole feeling a lot better. I had a couple of glimpses of Snowball; only from afar now the fence had been fixed and I hadn't risked going round there. Yet.

Tomasz bounded out after us, followed by a slightly more reluctant Henry. The boys started kicking the ball and I just watched them, rather than joining in, given that the ball was almost as big as me. Tomasz rushed into Aleksy, sending him flying, then he kicked the ball up into the air.

'Tommy, stop,' Aleksy said, rubbing his leg as he sat on the ground.

'Sorry, Aleksy, I didn't mean to hurt you.'

'The ball is gone,' Henry said, pointing at the fence. We all looked but the ball had disappeared.

'I am very cross,' Aleksy said to Tomasz as he picked himself up and, blinking back tears, made his way inside.

I followed him, leaving Tomasz and Henry outside. Everyone else was in the kitchen, chatting and sorting out food that smelt delicious, even with my reduced appetite.

'Mum, Tommy kicked the ball over the fence and he bashed into me.' Aleksy was a sensitive boy, and he rushed to his mother's side and into her arms.

'Which way did it go?' Jonathan asked.

'That side.' Aleksy pointed to the Snells'.

'Oh boy, they might not even answer the door.'

'Who's going to go?' Claire asked.

'You know after we all bonded over the missing Snowball we've barely seen them,' Jonathan said.

'Really?' Tomasz asked.

'I'll go,' Polly announced.

As Polly stood up to go, my heart leapt and I quickly stood up too. I definitely wasn't going to miss this opportunity.

We made our way next door, Polly striding along and me running to keep up with her. I was excited about the fact I had an excuse to maybe get a glimpse of Snowball. I hadn't seen her since she banished me, but I was also nervous at the idea of seeing her and how she might react.

Polly looked a bit anxious as she rang the doorbell. I could hear movement from inside the house, and then after what seemed like ages, the door slowly opened.

'Hello, Polly,' Daisy said with a smile as she opened the door. She turned round, shouting 'It's Polly.' We couldn't hear the response but no one else rushed to greet us. 'Sorry, Mum's tied up in the kitchen.' I hoped she didn't mean literally.

'Right, so anyway,' Polly started, her eyebrows a bit raised. 'My friend's little boy kicked the ball over your fence. I'm so sorry but I wondered if you wouldn't mind getting it for us.'

'Of course, no problem.' I was surprised that Daisy was quite so sunny, given how she'd been when I'd seen her previously. She hadn't closed the door when she went to get the ball, so I stood by Polly's feet looking in; but there was no sign of Snowball, and I couldn't help but feel disappointed. After a few minutes, we heard footsteps and then Daisy returned with Aleksy's ball.

'Thank you so much, love. He'll be relieved and I'll make sure we don't disturb you again.'

''S all right,' Daisy said, suddenly looking a bit coy. 'Can I ask you, are you a model?'

'No, not anymore, but I was before having two kids.' Polly laughed. 'And certainly not a supermodel, but I did a few magazines and catwalks in my time. Why, are you interested in that world?' Polly asked.

'I'd love it but Mum and Dad well …'

'Daisy, you have the height, and the looks, although I obviously don't know how you photograph. How old are you?'

'Sixteen.' Daisy was red-faced but I noticed that she was very pretty. I wonder why I hadn't noticed it before.

'Well, take my advice, get your exams first and then maybe think about it. It's a tough world. But if you're really interested and if your parents are OK, I can help with agencies.'

'Would you really?'

'Of course. But as I said, your parents have to agree to it, and don't do anything until after your GCSEs.'

We heard shouting from inside; it sounded like they were wondering what was keeping Daisy. She looked apologetic.

'Sorry, I better go, but I'll talk to Mum and Dad.'

'Thanks for the ball,' Polly said as Daisy closed the door. I was flooded with disappointment. I knew Snowball knew I was there, I could sense her, but she clearly didn't want to see me.

We walked down the path and back to mine in silence. As Claire opened the door, Aleksy rushed forward and looked delighted to see his ball.

'Don't kick it over again or it's lost.'

'It wasn't me, it was Tomasz,' Aleksy protested.

'OK, tell him to be more careful, love.' Polly ruffled his hair as she handed the ball over. She and Claire went into the kitchen. Everyone was sitting around the table. Martha was in the highchair that they brought over with them and when Polly sat down the food was served.

'How was it next door?' Jonathan asked.

'Honestly those poor people are like characters in a soap opera; everyone wondering what they are up to or why they are like they are! Anyway, Daisy answered the door, I didn't see anyone else.'

'I wish we knew what their deal was? What was she like with you?' Claire asked.

'Very sweet, wanted to know if I was a model. I said I'd help her if her parents were happy with it but I can't imagine they would be.'

'Do you think they might be like those secret people?' big Tomasz asked. I sat at Aleksy's feet and the children were all concentrating on their food; the adults seemed more keen to chat.

'What secret people?' Matt asked.

'You know something happens and they have to be new people and no one can know who they really are?' big Tomasz explained.

'Oh yes, those in witness protection!' Claire exclaimed.

'Well I guess it would explain why they don't want to see anyone.' Polly nodded.

'And why the police visit sometimes,' Jonathan added.

'Yes but if you're in witness protection you have to act normally so as not to raise suspicion surely?' Matt chipped in.

'Oh yeah.' They all reverted to looking as confused as they did when they started speculating.

After lunch had been cleared away, including my empty bowl, they all decided to go for a walk, as it was a cold but sunny day. As children were bundled into coats, and Matt fetched Martha's pushchair, I decided that as much fun as it had been I was glad for some time alone.

I bade them all goodbye and made my way to the back garden to sunbathe. As I jumped through the cat flap I was surprised to find a most unexpected visitor in my garden. Snowball.

I couldn't believe my eyes.

'Hi, why are you here?' I asked, taken aback.

'We had a deal. Or so I thought. Why did you come to the house before?'

She was as coldly hostile as ever, but beautiful with it too.

'Snowball, you can't blame me for that. I was helping Polly get Aleksy's ball back, but I have kept away the past few days.'

'Don't take me for a fool, Alfie.'

'I never would.'

She looked at me witheringly. OK, so maybe I was a bit, but you can't blame a cat for trying. 'Anyway, Daisy seemed really happy to see Polly.'

'She was.' Snowball looked a bit sad for a minute. I had found her weak spot; it was Daisy. 'But of course then when she spoke to her mum and dad they weren't happy. They kept telling her that modelling is so tough, and not many people make it. I mean she was happy for the first time in months; you'd think they might have been a bit more supportive.'

'Yes, you would. Why do you think the parents are doing that?'

'They're scared, Alfie, really scared. We all are. I know those horrible people with that nasty cat Salmon think we're bad, and I know everyone else thinks we're strange, but that's not it. We're scared. Nervous even, and on top of that we've lost the ability to trust.'

'Wow, that's a lot to deal with. What on earth has happened to ruin your family's trust like this?'

'I can't tell you, and you know why I can't,' she reprimanded me.

'Fair enough.' I needed to tread carefully, this was the nicest she had been to me and I didn't want to ruin that. 'I get it, Snowball, honestly I do, because I was in a bad place, I told you. There must be something we can do. You can't do it on your own.' I looked at her, her eyes were filled with sadness that I just wanted to take away from her. 'And it's the same for us cats. You need friends and I'm willing to be just that.'

She stood up and walked around in a circle, as if she was thinking about what I said. Then she looked at me again.

'You're a good cat, Alfie and I'm sorry I was so mean to you, but I have to do what my family wants me to do, and that means I have to keep away.'

'Are you sure you won't let me help?'

'For now I can't, sorry.' She looked at me. 'Honestly, Alfie, I really am sorry.'

I was speechless as I knew that somehow, in my little garden, something had changed. A switch had been flicked. And although I didn't know where that would lead, I felt we had taken a giant leap forward.

She turned and ran as she heard voices. My families were back and Snowball had disappeared in a puff of fluff.

★★★

'Alfie looks like the cat who got the cream,' Claire observed later when the others had all gone home. She was right, I couldn't get the grin off my face, ever since my encounter with Snowball. I know she didn't exactly furnish me with good news but I felt that had been our first truly friendly conversation. I couldn't be happier.

'Hey, if he looks like the cat who got the cream, then let's give him the cream. There's some left over from pudding.' As he winked, Claire giggled and I licked my lips. Moments like this, when life felt good, were priceless. And on top of that I had a big bowl of cream to enjoy.

-CHAPTER-
Twenty-Nine

'Do you fancy going to the park?' Tiger asked. We were lazing around at our patch at the end of the street. Our little gang – Elvis, Nellie, Rocky, and our newest member Tom – had been having a competition. We'd been stalking mice, but I lost as usual. Tom had won, although it was clear to us all that he was just trying to impress Tiger.

'Sorry but I need to go home, Claire's not herself,' I explained. 'Next time though.'

'I'll come to the park with you, Tiger,' Tom offered, gruffly. I tried not to grin.

'Oooooh,' Nellie teased.

'Shut up, Nellie. Come on, Tom, let's go.' Tiger stalked off without a backward glance and Tom followed. It was quite a sight to be seen. Tiger, confidently striding and the normally alpha male Tom, literally tottering after her. They did made a cute couple though, in a strange kind of way.

It was true that I was concerned about Claire. I worried that with the excitement of everything that was happening with Snowball, I was neglecting my own family. I had to do a mental inventory: Matt, Polly and the kids were definitely all right; Franceska and family, ditto; but I wasn't so sure about Claire and Jonathan.

While Jonathan was the same as always, the reliable man I loved so much, Claire was see-sawing between being calm and angry. One minute she would seem happy, the next she would be snapping at Jonathan, or crying. I really was worried about her. I knew she wanted a baby, but I didn't understand why she was behaving like this. Jonathan said to me the other day that he was walking on eggshells, and his patience – which wasn't great at the best of times – was being tested.

Whenever Jonathan asked her what was wrong she would snap 'nothing,' in an almost hateful way. I would try to make things better by snuggling up to her, but so often she would burst into tears and I was left thinking I'd only made things worse, even when I purred in my most relaxing way. Jonathan and I were at a loss as to how we could help Claire and fix this situation.

I loved Claire so much, I couldn't bear for her to be upset, although it seemed there was little I could do. I could see Jonathan didn't know what to do either. He was attentive, he was loving but he didn't smother her – Jonathan wasn't the smothering kind. He bought her flowers, which for some reason made her cross; she accused him of trying to 'buy' her whatever that meant? This crazy behaviour hadn't been going on long enough for me to be desperately worried but Claire seemed to be on a slippery slope leading her back to her self-destructive ways. Jonathan was like an innocent bystander, trying to save her but without any idea of whether or not he was doing the right thing. And I for one knew exactly how that felt.

I walked into the kitchen and it seemed my timing was impeccable. Claire was standing in front of a broken dish, sobbing. She sank to the floor, cradling her knees and sobbed even harder. I went over to her, brushing against her but she didn't even notice. Jonathan was nowhere to be seen. I didn't know what to do.

I needed to take matters into my own paws, so I made my way to Polly and Matt's. They were all there as I jumped through the cat flap and into their kitchen. The children were having something to eat and Matt was feeding Martha.

I miaowed loudly.

'Hi, Alfie,' Matt said, as he stopped spoon-feeding Martha. Martha immediately started to cry loudly, so he continued.

At times like this I wished I could talk. Instead, I used my loudest yowl. Henry jumped and dropped his food, Matt looked at me as did Polly.

'What's wrong?' Matt asked.

'Do you think something's really wrong?' Polly asked. I yowled again – of course there was something wrong. I put my head back through the cat flap to indicate that they needed to follow me to Claire's.

'Maybe I'll check Claire's?' Polly suggested. 'Can you hold the fort?'

'Sure thing.'

Polly stood up and headed out of the house. I followed her, keeping so close to her legs I was touching them. I wanted her to know I needed her, and this was the best way I could do that.

'Alfie, I'm going to trip over you,' she said, picking me up. She marched us to our front door and rang the doorbell. There was no answer. 'Is anyone home?' she asked. I miaowed the affirmative. She rang the bell again, her finger pressed on it insistently. Finally, Claire answered the door.

'Bloody hell,' Polly said as she looked at her, echoing my thoughts. Her face was streaked with tears, her hair was a mess and she looked terrible. It was as if she had morphed into someone else.

'Thanks, Pol,' Claire said, sarcastically, standing aside to let her in. Claire went to the living room and Polly followed her.

'Sorry.' Polly looked contrite. 'What's going on? Alfie came over, yelping and yowling, and I thought that maybe you were in trouble.'

'I am in trouble. I hate myself at the moment, and soon I'll drive Jonathan away. He's been working late every night this week.'

'What's that got to do with things?'

'He doesn't want to spend any time with me and who can blame him?'

'Don't be crazy! He loves you, anyone can see that.'

'He might have loved the old me but I've turned into some kind of mad woman that no one could love.' She burst into tears again. Polly left the room, returning with tissues, which she handed to Claire.

'What's really going on?' she asked, sitting down next to Claire on the sofa.

'I don't know. It's the baby thing. We've been trying for ages now, and I just can't help it but now, every time I get PMT I feel so horribly disappointed that I can't bear it. And this time, well this time is the worst ever. For a couple of weeks now I've just felt evil and I know my period is coming, which makes me feel even worse.'

'Claire, I don't want to make things worse but you can't have this every month.'

'I know, but what can I do? I want to kill someone one minute and I just can't stop sobbing the next.' To illustrate this she burst into tears. Polly hugged her.

'Listen, honey, this isn't right. PMT shouldn't be making you feel like this.'

'Well I do. There's probably something seriously wrong with me and I need to see a doctor. It's probably early onset menopause, knowing my luck. Oh and look at my complexion, I'm covered in teenage acne.'

'Claire, I don't think this is menopause or PMT,' Polly said gently.

'Oh my God, you mean it's something worse?'

'Since when were you such a hypochondriac? No, no!' Polly replied.

'Well what is it?' I've been pre-menstrual for a couple of weeks.'

'Claire, do you think...' Polly smiled. 'Claire, do you think you could be pregnant?'

Claire looked at Polly, thunderously. Not the reaction either of us were expecting.

'Please, sorry, I know how much you want to be, so don't hit me, but if you're not pregnant then you need to see a doctor about the uncontrollable mood-swings and the first thing they'll do is make you take a test.' Polly sounded so reasonable and calm. I was glad I'd fetched her.

'Oh God.' Claire looked at Polly, who displayed a glimmer of hope in her eyes. 'Shall I do one?' Claire was trembling.

'I take it you have some?' Polly asked.

'I've got about fifty in the bathroom.' That was my Claire – always well prepared.

She came downstairs a little while later. Polly was in the kitchen, having cleared up the broken bowl. Claire still looked terrible.

'Well?' Both Polly and I waited with bated breath.

'Positive.'

'You did a test?'

'I did four. Oh my, I'm pregnant. I'm actually pregnant!' Claire sounded shocked but with joy dancing across her face.

'Claire, you're having a baby!' Polly shouted, grabbing Claire and hugging her.

'Oh my God,' Jonathan said, as he appeared in the doorway. None of us had heard him come in, we were so caught up. I watched as a huge smile spread across his face. Then Polly laughed, and Claire finally smiled and as Jonathan grabbed her in a huge hug they both cried and laughed at the same time. Polly quietly snuck out, as did I; it was a moment for just the two of them.

We were going to be a proper family now! I was so excited, and relieved. Now Claire would be happy again. All she wanted was a baby and now it looked as if she was getting one. We were all getting one.

-CHAPTER-
Thirty

'**A**lfie, look,' Tiger said, gesturing to where Heather and Vic Goodwin stood on the pavement outside their house with a strange man. The man was wearing a suit and he didn't exactly look happy. I had gone to find Tiger to deliver the good news, whilst giving Jonathan and Claire some alone time.

'We need to see if we can find out what's going on,' I said, wondering if it was to do with the Snells.

'Leave it to me.' Tiger carefully crossed the road and hid under a car nearby. I didn't know whether to follow her but my decision was made for me when Salmon appeared, jumping onto a wall and looking right at me with his beady eyes. Luckily it seemed he hadn't seen Tiger. I would have to wait here and bide my time so as not to arouse suspicion.

The suited man walked off, crossed the road to number 48 and rang the bell. Now I was really worried. The Goodwins and Salmon watched the man, all wearing the same matching self-satisfied smiles. When she felt sure everyone was looking the other way, Tiger rejoined me and we went to my front garden, out of sight of the horrible Salmon.

'So …?' I pushed, desperate for information.

'It seems he's the Snells' landlord. The Goodwins said the family are up to no good, and although he assured them that there was nothing illegal going on in the house, they didn't believe him. It sounds as if they've literally been hounding him which is why he finally caved in and said he would go and see the Snells.'

'Do you think he's angry with the Snells?'

'I think he's more angry with the Goodwins. I heard him say they pay their rent on time, they're no trouble, although of course the Goodwins didn't agree with that. In the end he said he would speak with them and tell them that the neighbours were concerned. But that's all he's agreed to.'

'Oh good. I would hate the Goodwins' witch hunt to drive them out.'

'They won't give up though. I think they've far too much time on their hands and keep going on about the fact that if they have bad neighbours then the property prices will fall, whatever that means.'

'What do your family think?' I asked.

'Well, I've heard them speaking to the Goodwins and they seem to be easily led by them. I mean my family are great and all, but they like a quiet life. The Goodwins have convinced them that they will cause a massive disturbance on the street before too long, so they are ready to support them.'

We went back to the street to see if there were any developments. The Goodwins had gone, as had Salmon, but there was no sign of the man who was possibly inside the Snells' house now. I looked at Tiger.

'This feels like it's just a mess but one which could so easily be cleared up.'

'Is that your cat instinct?'

'Yes, but now I have to go home, because I think it's probably time for a celebratory dinner.'

'You mean they might give you some nice fish because of the baby.'

'I'm hoping so.'

'Right, well call for me tomorrow and we can see what's happening.'

'Oh, by the way, how was your trip to the park with Tom?' I asked. Tiger hadn't been forthcoming with information so far.

'Yeah, fine thanks,' she replied but refused to say more before she ran off.

I was right, as soon as I got home, Jonathan gave me some fish. As I ate, he started making dinner, while Claire sat at the table.

'You know,' Claire started, 'it's still early days. I know Polly knows, so Matt will too, which means we'll have to tell Franceska and Tomasz, but perhaps we should hold off telling anyone else, just yet.'

'Whatever you want, darling. But you need to see a doctor anyway, just to get the ball rolling, and then we can take it from there.' Jonathan sounded more excited than I had ever heard him, I thought.

'Yes, I'll call them first thing. I am so unbelievably happy, Jonathan, but I really worry that something might go wrong.'

'Nothing will go wrong, Claire. You do know that, deep down, don't you?' I miaowed, because I knew deep down that it would all be all right.

Claire's worried face transformed and she giggled unexpectedly, she actually giggled.

'You know what, I do. Sometimes I think that I can't be this lucky. To have found you, and this gorgeous house, a job I love, Alfie of course, our friends and now the baby. But then also, deep down, I think that this is all meant to be. This happiness, I deserve it, I earned it, and so I need to start enjoying it rather than worrying.'

'My goodness, Claire! How long have I been telling you this? At last you see it for yourself.' Jonathan came over and kissed the top of her head.

'Yeah I know, Mr Right all the time,' she teased. 'Faith, belief in happiness, doesn't come easy to me, but it will now, I promise. I love you and we're going to be a wonderful family.'

Hoping that included me, I gently jumped up onto Claire's lap. She picked me up and kissed my nose. 'I may be having a baby but I will always love you, Alfie,' she said, happiness radiating from her. 'You'll always be my baby too.' I smiled, I would always be loved, and I knew that as a certainty.

-CHAPTER-
Thirty-One

Polly's mum was visiting – babysitting – and Polly and Matt were in Claire and Jonathan's living room. They were all drinking apart from Claire who had sworn off wine until after the baby was born.

'So the doctor said you could be over two months pregnant?' Polly asked.

'Yes, it looks like it, but it's still early days.'

'Be confident, and calm, that's the most important thing. And be thankful that you're not too sick!'

'I will, and the exciting thing is that there won't be that long between mine and Tasha's babies – Martha isn't that much older really in the whole scheme of things.'

'Are you going to find out the sex?'

'I think so. I'm not one for surprises but Jonathan is convinced it's a boy and is already calling him "he". He thinks that he, Alfie and the baby are going to make this a totally male-dominated household.'

'He's happy, isn't he?' Polly laughed.

'So happy! Isn't it great to see a gruff man showing his caring side. I mean I know how much he loves Alfie, but now, well, with this it's just gorgeous.'

'And you are a fluffy marshmallow. Right let's say something horrible before I go too soft.' They laughed, and the doorbell rang.

'Expecting anyone?' Jonathan asked.

'No, Frankie's with the boys and Tomasz couldn't get off work.' Claire got up to answer the door. I went with her and was horrified to see the Goodwins on the doorstep. What a way to ruin our little celebration.

'Hi,' Claire said nervously. 'I don't mean to be rude but we've kind of got company.'

'Well this won't take long,' Heather said, almost sweeping her aside. Vic followed, grinning his sinister grin.

'Oh good,' he said as he entered the living room. 'Matt and Polly too.'

They were all struck dumb.

'Why are you wearing Christmas jumpers? It's June?' Jonathan finally asked after scrabbling about for something to say. Jonathan was right, their jumpers had snowmen on them. If anyone was a danger to this street it was them.

'Oh they're for our annual Christmas card. Salmon has a jumper the same,' Vic explained.

'Yes, we like to get organized, so the photographer came today. We haven't had time to change yet.'

'Erm, lovely ...' Polly arched an eyebrow, looking a bit lost for words.

'What can we do for you?' Claire asked, grabbing Jonathan's arm.

'It's about the Snells.'

'Of course it is.' Jonathan rolled his eyes.

'We've spoken to the landlord, but to no avail. He insists they're paying rent and are not criminals, therefore they're free to live there.'

'Great, so can we draw a line under this then?' Claire asked.

'No, no, I'm afraid we cannot. This street is a good street and I saw the daughter with a cigarette the other day.'

'That's not illegal.'

'It's actually pretty normal teenage behaviour,' Jonathan chipped in.

'No but it is indicative of the degenerative nature of youth. That family is rotten to the core. They won't meet us, so they obviously have something to hide. We will not stand for it.' Vic sounded determined as he flashed his scary smile.

'I really think you need to let this go,' Matt started. 'There is no need for a witch hunt, they haven't hurt anyone and just because the police have been round a couple of times, doesn't mean that they're a band of criminals. That could be anything.'

'I sometimes wonder if you people take Edgar Road seriously,' Heather said, sounding annoyed.

Vic spoke. 'She's right. Anyway, we've told the landlord that we are going to start a petition against them and if everyone in the street signs they'll have no choice but to leave,' Vic added.

'My God, you're going to hound potentially innocent people from their home? Even when they have kids?' Jonathan sounded angry and I was proud of him.

'All they need to do is to tell us why they are hiding from us. Now will you sign our petition or not?' They sounded hostile.

'You know what, we've humoured you long enough. We come to your very long meetings, and what do they achieve? Nothing! They're generally just a load of hot air.' Jonathan stood now but still kept a bit of distance between him and the Goodwins.

'Hours of hot air,' Matt supported, looking like a man who would never get those hours back again.

'But we won't see this neighbourhood becoming unwelcoming and nasty, which is what is happening thanks to you two. You've taken against people you don't know for reasons of your own imagining. No, we won't be signing your petition and unless you decide to be more reasonable we won't be coming to your meetings again,' Jonathan finished.

'How dare you!' Vic shouted.

'Hey, let's be calm about this,' Polly started. 'None of us are disputing that the family's behaviour is a little strange but we've spoken to Karen and Tim and we feel confident that they're simply a family in turmoil. And that's the only reason why they're so intent on keeping themselves to themselves.'

'Oh, Polly, you are young and naïve. You've let yourself be taken in by these people. Listen to our experience and trust us.' Heather sounded so patronizing.

'You're being ridiculous.' Jonathan lost his temper again. 'We'll have no part in what you're doing, so please leave my house and leave us alone. Blimey, the Snells have got the right idea.'

'It's a shame you own your homes otherwise we would have you evicted from the street too,' Vic said, shouting back at Jonathan.

I cowered under the seat; both men sounded quite aggressive.

'And don't think you will get one of our special Christmas cards this year either,' Heather added before they stormed out.

After everyone was sure they'd gone, Claire started laughing. 'My God, the ultimate punishment – no Christmas card!'

'I wish I could have been that photographer,' Polly said, tears of laugher rolling down her cheeks.

'Imagine, them and the cat in those jumpers?' Claire was almost doubled up.

'Where do you even get human and cat matching jumpers?' Matt asked.

'Oh she probably knits them,' Polly added.

'Hey, honey we could do that next year,' Jonathan suggested. 'Me, you, Alfie and the baby all in the same jumpers.'

'Somehow I don't think your relatives would get the irony,' Claire said.

'Now who said I was trying to be ironic?' Jonathan asked.

-CHAPTER-
Thirty-Two

L ove makes the world go round. If you look, you see it; snap-shots of love, everywhere you go. Especially on Edgar Road.

In a smile, a look, a gesture, you can feel and see love. It radiates a power that envelops everyone it touches. It wraps you up and keeps you safe and warm. You see the world a bit brighter, the sun feels warmer, the flowers look more colourful, and you see beauty everywhere.

Matt, Polly and the children all showed this love; Claire and Jonathan more than ever now; and it was obvious how much Franceska and Tomasz loved each other and their children. And they all loved me. Even the Goodwins gave off a feeling of love to each other, although it was strange they seemed to derive pleasure from meddling in other people's lives, but it was clear they loved each other and Salmon in their funny matching-jumper-kind-of-way.

Another month had passed since Tiger and Tom had started hanging out and they were looking almost loving, and, although it was clear that Tom was keener, the way Tiger acted when he was around suggested she was falling for his rather odd charms. So that left me. I loved so many people and cats, but of course the romantic part of my heart was reserved for Snowball.

There were many types of love, I learnt. The happy kind, that surrounded us and the sad kind that surrounded Snowball and the Snells. I knew they all loved each other but they were lost and theirs wasn't happy love, it was sad love. I had to do something about it, I knew, not least because I needed to win Snowball's heart. Although that probably makes it sound more selfish than it is, because I also love helping people – you see love can mean so much, it really does make the world go round.

Because Jonathan had stood up to the Goodwins they had become even more determined in their irrational dislike of the Snells. Tiger reported that they had indeed started a petition to get them to move from the road, and they were taking it door to door on our long street. It was ridiculous and the thing was never going to work, because most of the residents of Edgar Road wouldn't even know who the Snells were. We knew a few neighbours to wave at but even the dreaded Neighbourhood Watch meetings only attracted a fraction of the very long street.

What worried me was what I had heard Jonathan and Claire talking about. If the Snells were indeed vulnerable in any way then they would be made even more so if they felt unwelcome. They might even move to another house for a quiet life and that meant they would take my Snowball with them. Despite the fact there was no actual threat from the Goodwins the upset their action caused could do a lot of harm nonetheless.

In lieu of knowing how to fix everything, it was time for me to make a 'grand gesture'. I had seen this, both on television and in real life. A grand gesture was something one did to show your loved one how much you loved them, although it usually involved some kind of sacrifice.

It was time for me to do a grand gesture for Snowball. I needed to woo her. I needed to show her that I meant what I said, and that she wasn't alone. I had barely seen her since that time in the garden a few weeks ago, although I had tried to; she was proving ever more elusive, forcing me to step up my efforts.

I ruled out music, and crossed poetry off my list too as cats aren't great at reciting it. I could bring her a few gifts but that definitely wasn't special enough. I had no one to consult either; if I asked Tiger she would give me one of her withering looks and probably laugh at me. So, it was just down to me and I had to remember I was a cat. We might be resourceful but we don't quite have the *resources* of humans.

I decided to involve flowers, which all humans seemed to use to woo their women. I thought about the lovely flowers in Polly's front garden. Surely she could spare a couple of them for me?

I set out to pick some flowers, my plan still hazy but I felt confident that it would come to me. As I poked around in the flower beds, I realized picking flowers wasn't as easy as it looked. I tried to swipe the flowers with my paw but they just bounced back. Then I tried to scratch at them but that just served to make petals fall off. I tried to get a few, but that wasn't working, so there was nothing for it, I would have to dig. Digging was hard work – after all, I'm not some hapless dog – and I was beginning to feel as if this wasn't one of my better ideas, but finally I managed to dig deep enough to grab the flowers by the roots. Sitting, I then used both paws and my mouth to yank them from the ground.

I then faced the problem of how to carry them. All I had available to me was my mouth, so I laid them down, bent my head and picked them up, trying to ignore the earthy taste. I had to admit they didn't look quite as good as they had in the ground by the time I made my way to Snowball's house. I hoped that what Claire often said was true; it was the thought that counts.

Snowball's back garden was deserted, as was the downstairs

of the house. I wanted to lay the flowers down but then how would she know that they were from me? I wondered what to do as these slightly destroyed flowers now didn't feel like such a grand gesture. I looked up at the tree that stood proudly in the garden and I had an idea. If I was in the tree when she saw me, I could climb down and present her with the flowers making the gesture even grander!

I wasn't the most practised climber but I was a very determined cat so I set off. Climbing with flowers in my mouth was actually harder than walking with them, but I clenched my teeth and got on with it. I didn't look down until I reached the second branch. It wasn't too high but definitely high enough, I decided, as I settled down to wait for Snowball.

It was actually really pleasant up there, I decided, as I surveyed my view. I couldn't see into the upstairs of the house because all the curtains were closed but I watched some birds, who seemed to be aiming for me but swerved at the last minute and darted off. My jaw started to ache from clenching onto the flowers but if I let go now, they would be lost. As time wore on, I wanted to move but couldn't, and as it grew colder and colder it eventually started to rain.

It had been sunny when I set out, but the sky darkened, the heavens opened and a rain shower ensued. As I felt my fur begin to droop I was beginning to think that this grand gesture wasn't actually such a good idea. Then Snowball appeared from her cat flap.

'What on earth are you doing?' she asked, but she was smiling, or actually laughing at the sight of me, drenched to the skin and now clinging to the branch with cold.

Still, I might be soaking wet but now it was time for me to go down and present the flowers as planned. And ta da!

I then met the next flaw in my plan as I realized that my back legs had seized up. My old injury had returned, just as it often did when it rained. I really hadn't thought this through. I had spent too long in one position, and I needed to start wiggling them. The only problem was I was in a tree. With flowers in my mouth. What was a cat to do?

'Alfie, are you OK?' Snowball said, beginning to look concerned. I had no choice, I opened my mouth and the flowers fluttered to the ground. One of them landed on Snowball's head. So I guess she got the idea at least. She didn't look as pleased as I'd hoped though, as she shook the flowers off which were dripping wet too.

'Sorry, but they were for you.'

'Alfie, what on earth are you doing?'

'Well, I had this idea that I'd get you flowers, which by the way isn't as easy as it looks for a cat. And then I was going to sit up here and wait for you and then jump down and present you with them.'

'Why on earth would you do that?'

'It works for humans.' I was in pain and beginning to feel a bit grumpy.

'But now?' Snowball asked.

'Well I have this problem with my back legs sometimes, so it seems I might be a bit stuck.'

'Stuck?'

'Yes, as in I can't move.'

I tried to wriggle again but my back legs were still too stiff to be much use.

'Oh, Alfie, what can I do?' At least she had softened towards me, although she hadn't picked up the flowers. Or said thank you come to think of it.

There is this urban myth that cats are always being rescued by firemen. It does happen for the less intellectual of our kind, but not as much as people would have you think as it's the ultimate humiliation for a cat.

'Would you mind finding my friend Tiger?' I asked, at a loss. I wasn't sure what she could do but she understood my physical limitations and might be able to help.

'OK, I guess I can try. Although this rain doesn't suit me.'

I told Snowball where she might find her and she reluctantly trotted off. I tried to stretch out but my legs just weren't having it. I was cold, wet and unable to move, my grand gesture slowly becoming one of my worst ideas ever.

It seemed forever before I saw Tiger following Snowball into the back yard. She took one look at me and laughed.

'Thanks,' I said. The rain had stopped as suddenly as it had started, so that was something.

'What on earth are you doing?'

'I'm stuck. That's all you need to know, my back legs have seized up.' I saw Tiger look at me, then at Snowball and finally at the sad-looking flowers.

'Oh, Alfie, I'll come up. You never were very good at climbing trees.' Tiger quickly climbed the tree and joined me whilst Snowball sat on the ground looking at us.

'You can't move at all?' Tiger asked, sounding concerned finally.

'My legs have gone all stiff. I've tried to wriggle but I don't think I can. Tiger, promise me that whatever you do you won't let them call the fire brigade.'

'What if it means you have to stay up here forever?'

'Tiger, you were supposed to help.'

'I know but what can I do? I don't think I can carry you down, you might have to jump.'

'But it's too far and if I land on my back legs it'll be worse.'

'Alfie, why do you insist on doing all these stupid things?'

'Tiger, you're not helping.'

'Do you guys maybe want to stop arguing and tell me what I can do?' Snowball asked but for once we were both lost for words; and ideas.

The patio doors suddenly opened and Christopher walked out. He looked at Snowball, then up at the tree. Tiger looked at me.

'He'll save you,' she whispered.

'You get down and then he'll know I'm stuck,' I suggested. Tiger, showing an agility I could only envy, quickly climbed down from the tree. She joined Snowball.

'So you've got friends, then, Snowball? More than I have,' Christopher said, looking and sounding glum. 'Is that Alfie up there?' he asked.

Snowball miaowed.

'Is he stuck?'

She miaowed again. Christopher smiled.

'Don't worry, mate, I'll get you.' He tried to climb up but I was a bit too high for him.

'Damn it, I can't get up there,' he said to himself and I felt a little more petrified. He went to the shed and took something out. When I looked I almost cried with relief, it was a ladder.

'All rescued, Alfie,' Christopher said a little while later, looking pleased with himself as he placed me gently on the wet ground. I purred and nuzzled into his legs with gratitude. He put the ladder back in the shed. I stretched and my legs started to regain some movement.

'I can't wait to tell everyone,' he said, and I saw a glimpse of the boy underneath the surly teenager.

'What was that all about?' Snowball asked when he'd gone, narrowing her eyes at me.

'It was my way of cheering you up. Flowers and me up a tree. My grand gesture,' I explained. When I said it out loud it didn't make as much sense as it had in my head.

Tiger looked at Snowball and smiled.

'It didn't quite go to plan,' Tiger teased.

'No, not exactly,' I replied.

'But it was a nice thought. Right, come on, Alfie, let's get you home,' Tiger said. She was right, I was loath to leave Snowball but I needed to go dry off and rest my legs somewhere warm and comfortable.

'OK. Sorry about the …' I started to say to Snowball but she gave me an affectionate flick of her tail.

''S all right,' she replied, neck pulled in coyly. I felt a prickle in my whiskers. I reluctantly started walking away.

'You know what?' Tiger said to Snowball. 'Alfie might be a bit of an idiot at times, with all these harebrained schemes, but you know you could do a lot worse.'

Snowball smiled, actually smiled, in response.

I grinned to myself as I limped home.

CHAPTER
Thirty-Three

My leg stiffness had eased and I was mobile again by the next morning. I resolved to take it easy for a day or two, to give myself thinking time. I was feeling reflective, the way I always did when my legs ached and I was reminded of the things that had happened in my past. I would think about events, cats and people in my life, past and present.

I felt lucky; my world was full of colour at the moment and my families were all thriving. Claire's 'jigsaw' was complete, along with Jonathan's, and I had rarely seen two happier people. This baby, when it was born, would be the most wanted and most doted on baby, and as long as they didn't forget me I was all for it. After all, it wouldn't be like having a new friend, it would be like having a new sibling for me, a human sibling. I would have to work very hard taking care of it as I would be the older brother from now on. The way Aleksy would always look out for little Tomasz, or Henry for Martha.

I took a long time to perform my morning ablutions, and then I thought about going to see Tiger. I wasn't planning on going on one of our usual long walks but a bit of exercise was good for me. I slid out of the cat flap and found myself face to face with Snowball.

'Hi,' I said, suddenly feeling shy at her unexpected appearance.

'Hello, Alfie. I thought I would see how you are after yesterday.'

'That's sweet,' I replied. 'But I'm good thank you. Feel a bit silly that it all went a bit …'

'Wrong? Yes it did, but it did make me smile. And Christopher was so animated last night, after rescuing you; it was as if you did it as a favour just for him.'

'Wish I'd thought of that really.' I said, thinking that I really did. It would have saved me having to dig up Polly's flower bed.

'Well, you always said you could help, and you did a bit. Anyway, I wondered if you wanted to go for a walk?'

'With you?' I was shocked; was she asking me on a date?

'Yes, of course with me. I thought maybe we could talk.'

'OK, but can we take it slowly? I'm still aching a bit.' I wasn't going to pretend to be macho; that would only lead to more trouble.

'No problem.' We looked at each other and I felt my whiskers tingle again. I hoped my legs weren't shaking as we set off. I didn't want to bump into any other cats, so I led Snowball in the direction of the park.

'Have you been to the park before?' I asked.

'No, I tend not to go out much at the moment – I prefer to stay close to home.'

'Where did you live before this?' I asked.

'In Kent, it's not that far from London but we lived in a really big house, with all this land around us.'

'Our houses are quite big,' I exclaimed. My first home was much smaller than Jonathan's house, and his was the biggest house I had ever been in.

'I guess, but the problem is that they're not all that large compared to what we had. I barely left my garden. It could take all day to explore it, it was that big. And there were flower beds and trees and even a lake. It was so much fun.'

'Really? So nothing like here?' I could only imagine what Snowball was used to, it sounded amazing.

'No, nothing like here. We didn't have neighbours so close, we had loads of space around us. And the house was bigger too. Far too big to be honest. I could go for hours without seeing anyone, despite the fact we lived together.'

'Why did they have such a big house?'

'I don't know, it's a human thing. They had a lot of money, and people who have a lot of money often have big houses. They had more than two cars too. Daisy and Christopher went to schools that they had to pay for and Karen, well you might find it hard to believe, but she had so many clothes they could barely fit in her wardrobe! She looked glamorous all the time. She did work part-time though as she never liked just being at home. Not like now.'

'What do you mean?'

'She works all the time, in a hospital, any shifts she can get as she's the only one earning money.' Snowball looked sad, but we had reached the park.

'Come on, I'll show you the best bushes.' I led her over and we crawled under a bush, it was really quite nice being there, alone together. It felt quite intimate as the leaves shadowed us and we sat side by side.

'So what happened to it all?'

'I shouldn't be telling you any of this.'

'I know, but I did get stuck up a tree for you.' I smiled and tried to nuzzle her; she didn't push me away, but she did look a bit embarrassed.

'Right, well, anyway, we had lots of money because Tim is very clever with computers and he had a company, which was very successful. He worked a lot, mind you, and Karen always moaned that she never saw him. But they went on these exotic holidays and when they did I had to stay in a cat hotel, which I wasn't that keen on to be honest, but they would always come back happy.'

'A cat hotel?' I had never heard of such a thing.

'Yes, you had to sleep in your own cage and you got fed but there were other cats and you didn't get half the attention you get at home.'

'Sounds like the vet to me.'

'Um, not exactly. Anyway there was this other man, Simon, he was Tim's business partner but also his best friend. He was the best man at their wedding, there are photos of him; I mean there were. And the children called him Uncle Simon. He didn't have any children of his own, but he always had a different girlfriend and Karen never liked them.' Snowball rolled over, and sighed.

'Sounds a bit like how Jonathan used to be before Claire,' I said.

'Anyway, Simon was always around. He and Tim were so close and he trusted him. But then this thing happened.'

'Go on.' I could barely wait.

'Simon turned out to be bad. Really bad. He managed to do something called fraud and he took off with all their money.'

'How on earth did he do that?' I asked, not really comprehending.

'I don't exactly know how he did it but he left the company bankrupt, which means totally broken I think. He left Tim in a huge mess.'

'So Tim didn't suspect anything?'

'No, he trusted Simon. But he was left owing a lot of money and he had to shut down the business. It was a huge mess. The police are trying to find him but according to Tim and Karen, even if they do it won't make things right again.'

'I'm horrified that someone could do that.'

It was beginning to make a bit of sense as to why the Snells were so secretive and unwilling to let anyone in. No wonder they didn't trust anyone.

'It got worse though. Not only did they lose everything and have to move here but they also lost all their friends. Some people pointed the finger at Tim; although he lost everything they still thought he'd done something bad. People turned their backs on them as soon as they found out they were poor, too. It was awful. All those people who came round for parties, drank that fizzy wine, and ate our food, wouldn't even answer their phones to Tim or Karen. They were forced to sell their house, the kids had to leave their expensive schools, and their friends abandoned them too. That was when Karen got a job near here so they moved to Edgar Road.'

'But why did they think Tim was involved?' I asked, trying to clarify.

'People are judgemental, Alfie. But he is totally innocent and when they moved here he was too terrified to make friends in case they thought he was a criminal.'

'The irony is that by refusing to befriend anyone on the street the Goodwins think exactly that.'

'I know but he's too affected by everything that's happened to think straight. They all are.'

'It's a sad story. Although I will never understand why humans value money so highly, above everything else. Cats don't have any and look how happy we are. All we need is a butterfly to chase, a warm fire to come home to, and a loving lap to sit on.'

'I don't understand either.'

'And they say us cats are superficial! But when it comes down to it, we're more loyal than most of them.'

'I agree, Alfie.' Snowball looked at me, and I couldn't stop my heart from pounding. 'So now you know what happened,' she continued. 'The police come round because of Simon. But Karen and Tim are still so depressed and so hurt, that they won't let themselves meet anyone. They've put their guard up, and now the Goodwins are making everything so much worse, just when they thought they might be able to get their lives back on track.'

'That's the thing, when you're down, sometimes you can't see anything good.'

'No, and I couldn't either for a time. I'm worried for the kids. Chris is being teased at his new school because he came from a posh school. But he's good at football, so if he would just get involved in that he would be OK. He refuses to though. And Daisy is popular because she's pretty. To be honest, she has always been a bit of princess so she struggles with the change in her lifestyle, although as Karen points out on a regular basis, she is luckier than so many people.'

'And she is – you all are – but then if you have something and it gets taken away, it's totally natural to miss it.'

I thought about what Dustbin had said about how some people didn't have homes and it wasn't their choice. That made me feel so sad. 'Some people don't have any home, let alone a nice one like yours,' I said, gently.

'I know, you're right, but I miss it too. My old life, my garden. I was miserable and sad when I first came here, and I didn't want to see anyone or make any friends.'

'Really, I'd never have known,' I joked.

'Yes, but then this cat called Alfie came along and he wouldn't take no for an answer.'

'And are you glad I wouldn't?' I asked, suddenly feeling quite emotional. Snowball snuggled up next to me; her warmth made me feel as if I was made of gold. I nuzzled into her neck.

'Yes, I think I just might be,' she replied.

Forget my sore legs, after hearing that I floated on air everywhere for the rest of the day.

-CHAPTER-
Thirty-Four

'Well, you know I'd go and see them, but the last time I did I made things worse, and I don't think they'd even open the door for me,' Jonathan said.

Polly and Matt had popped in with the children on their way home, although it was bedtime. Claire was giving Martha a cuddle, Henry and I were playing with a plastic ball as they spoke.

'I don't think they'll let any of us in. But you know we have to try to do something.'

'We could write them a note,' Claire suggested.

'Not a bad idea,' Polly agreed.

I was trying to concentrate on what everyone was saying, but it was difficult as my mind kept drifting back to the previous day with Snowball. After our lovely date, I slept beautifully and had lots of wonderful dreams. I had never been in love like this and until yesterday it was all one-sided. She hadn't exactly given in totally to my charms but she had softened towards me and when I walked her to her back door, we had a little nose rub. I asked her when I would see her again but she had only said, soon. She seemed to have put a bit of her guard back up, although not totally. I just had to be patient.

As I listened to what was going on around me, it turned out that Polly had had another run-in with the Goodwins earlier.

I hadn't seen Snowball today and I now found out why. Polly was upset. On her way back from dropping Henry off at nursery she ran into the Goodwins and two police officers outside the Snells' house. According to her, the Goodwins were wearing camouflage clothes – like they wear in the army – and said they had been undercover watching the Snells' house. The police were trying to explain they were here to see the Snells but the Goodwins kept trying to pump them for information. Polly said they were crazy and she almost expected the police to arrest them for harassment.

Heather and Vic were interrogating the police – apparently in normal circumstances it's the other way round. The police officers told them they couldn't say anything, although the Goodwins kept badgering them about the Snells being part of the criminal underworld, telling them about their petition, on which they had managed, somehow, to get more than twenty signatures. Polly stepped in at this point and said that they needed to be left alone. The Goodwins accused Polly of aiding and abetting and the police looked at her with sympathy as they finally managed to get away and headed into to the Snells' house.

'Quick, back to our vantage point,' Heather had said as they both ran to watch from behind a bush in their front garden.

Polly had gone home, fuming.

'It is quite comical when you think of it,' Jonathan said. 'I mean they're now dressing up like a bush to get to the bottom of something that probably doesn't have a bottom.'

'We all know they can't make them leave, but it must be upsetting to have a vendetta against you, no matter how ridiculous the perpetrators. I just think they should be told that we don't feel the same way the Goodwins do, and we want to lend any support we can. We need to show them that not everyone is as horrible as that pair.' Polly was incensed and I loved her for it.

'I agree,' Claire said. 'Let's get a letter done tonight and we can all sign it.'

'Right, Matt. Put the kids to bed and I'll write this letter with Claire now.'

'In that case, Jonathan, you can carry one of them home with me. And have a beer when we've put them down.'

'Sounds like a good plan to me,' Jonathan agreed. Claire and Polly both rolled their eyes.

I purred as loudly as I could to give them my approval, although I wasn't sure they got it. This was perfect. What the Snells needed to know was that they did have support. After what I had heard, about how vulnerable the family was, I really did worry the Goodwins could actually hurt them. I couldn't wait to tell Snowball, and to see her again of course.

I decided to take a chance as the women finished writing the letter and Polly delivered it on the way home. I headed next door too, going over the fence, praying it wouldn't hurt my legs. I went over to the patio doors but they had pulled blinds across. I moved over to the cat flap and I chanced things by putting my head through. Although I could smell Snowball, and I enjoyed taking a moment to breathe in her scent, there was no sign of her. I lay down. It was night but it was still quite light as I found a spot to wait.

I thought I heard a loud voice and then I heard a door slam. Then another one. Then I heard a strange sound, followed by miaowing, and more door slamming. I knew I shouldn't, I knew this was a bad time and no one wanted me there, but I couldn't help myself. Without thinking it through, I hopped through the cat flap and into the kitchen, which was shrouded in darkness. The house was empty. Snowball wasn't there. I looked everywhere – upstairs, downstairs – she was nowhere to be seen. What if something was wrong?

I knew it was wrong to break into someone's house, but I had to wait for them to come back. What if they had had enough and decided to flee regardless? I felt panic. What if I never saw Snowball again? I curled up under an armchair in the living room trying to control my fear. I felt as if I had been there for years before I heard the pitter patter of paws.

'Alfie!' Snowball exclaimed. 'What are you doing under the chair?'

'I was worried.'

'About what?'

'I thought you'd gone. Polly told me about the Goodwins and the police today and then Claire and Polly wrote a letter to you all to say we supported you. But I heard shouting and door slamming and thought you must have fled. I thought I'd never see you again. I was so worried I had to wait here. I couldn't risk leaving.'

'Blimey, Alfie, you have got an overactive imagination.'

'Well, yes perhaps I do, but look at you; yesterday you were all doom and gloom and today you seem different.'

'I was actually out looking for you! So guess what happened? The police came to say they had Simon. Although they might not get the money back, Tim will get his reputation restored and Simon will go to prison. My family are so much happier.

'Karen picked up the letter from your family, read it to Tim and they both hugged. Then the kids, well, with a bit of prompting from me, asked their parents if maybe things could go back to normal a bit. Their first act of normality was that they went out to get a take-away, together as a family. I was so happy I ran round to find you but you're here after all!'

'So what was all that shouting?'

'Well they were quite loud admittedly, but happy loud.'

'Oh, I feel like a total fool now.'

'You, Alfie, *are* a fool, a soppy fool.'

It was too late for me to leave before the front door opened and chatter flooded in, happy, lively chatter. Snowball smiled.

'Come on, you might as well meet them all properly.'

'Won't they be cross?'

'Today they wouldn't mind if you were a lion.'

I followed Snowball into the kitchen where the family were dishing up food and pouring drinks.

'Wish it could be Champagne, darling,' Tim said, as he handed Karen a glass of wine.

'I think we've had enough Champagne to last a lifetime, don't you?' she replied, smiling.

'Can I have some wine?' Daisy asked.

'A small glass,' her father replied, pouring her one.

'What about me?' Christopher asked.

'Oi, Daisy's sixteen, but you're only fourteen! 'Fraid not.' Tim ruffled his son's hair affectionately.

You would think it was a totally different family to look at them and I smiled at Snowball, who couldn't stop grinning at me.

'Is that the cat from next door?' Karen asked, spotting me.

'Yes, it's Alfie,' Christopher replied. 'Remember I told you I rescued him? I think he and Snowball are friends.'

'Even the cat next door is nice, then,' Karen mused. 'I was touched by that note and I feel quite bad for acting like a total nutcase in front of them, but I'm not sure I'm ready to tell everyone what we've been through.'

'I agree, it's still so raw,' said Tim.

'We still probably need a bit of time,' Karen said.

'Not to mention getting the dreaded Goodwins out of our hair. Did you hear the police say they were hiding in bushes trying to catch us out?'

'Clearly bonkers,' Daisy said.

'Yes, but I'm not ready to deal with them yet.' Karen sounded upset.

'Kids, Karen, I would like to say that I am really sorry for how bad things have been. I know moving was awful and adjusting to new schools, but now that Simon's been caught, I do feel that we might start to get back to normal. Well, a new kind of normal anyway.'

Tim looked sad again. I could see there had been a giant step forward but it wasn't quite giant enough.

Quietly, Snowball led me outside.

'Wow, things have changed quickly,' Snowball exclaimed when we were alone. 'I know Tim will never forgive himself for trusting Simon, but at least now he's been caught, it'll make him feel there's some justice.'

'Do you think they'll get the money back?'

'I think it's probably long gone. It was spent on bad investments and gambles from what I heard, but they have a home. It might not be what we were used to but it's better than many people have, you taught me that.'

'Everyone seemed happier. Well, apart from Christopher,' I pointed out.

'He's still missing his old life. I don't think he's made friends at school; I haven't seen him with anyone and he seems so withdrawn, more than any of the others. I'm Daisy's cat and Christopher doesn't like me half the time. Whenever he rows with his sister, he seems to blame me.'

'Is he mean to you?' I asked.

'Not really, just says the odd thing, calls me a scraggy moggy when he's really annoyed but I know deep down he doesn't mean it. He pretends not to like Daisy but deep down he loves her too,' Snowball explained.

'I think we need to get my families and yours together. Honestly, it'll really make yours feel welcome and wanted.'

'They might, one day. But I am glad I met you, Alfie.' Snowball nuzzled my neck and I felt like a million dollars.

CHAPTER
Thirty-Five

'Goodness, this is a bit like when Claire and Jonathan go out with Matt and Polly,' I said.

Three faces looked at me. Tiger, Tom, Snowball and I were at the park, playing in the flower beds. It was like a double date, I thought. Although for now Snowball was in the friend zone, I knew it was only a matter of time before we became more romantic.

Tiger wasn't exactly romantic towards Tom, but he followed her around like a lovesick puppy. She obviously liked him but she was, like Snowball, playing a bit hard to get. However, we were spending a very pleasant afternoon together so I wasn't complaining. Surprisingly, Tiger and Snowball had hit it off and Tom was definitely more charming than we had ever known him. I could see us becoming a tight little unit which made me feel more content than ever.

Although there was nothing wrong with my life before, having Snowball come into it had definitely added another dimension. My eyes shone a bit brighter, my smile was a bit wider, and when I slept, my dreams were filled with happiness.

And Snowball: her slow thaw towards me had accelerated at great speed – next stop love. Her family were also slowly thawing. I had seen quite a bit of them. Snowball said I was always welcome, so I had kind of added them to my list of homes, despite being there the least. I wanted them to meet my families, become friends, which is what a doorstep cat wants more than anything: to bring people together. Despite the fact they were happier and had been pleased to receive Claire and Polly's note, they hadn't rushed round with open arms. I understood. When you're hurt like that, when you lose everything and especially with betrayal added into the mix it takes time to heal and gain back the confidence to trust new people.

We still needed to find a way to get them to be friends the way we were. Gathered in the park, it seemed a good time to try to come up with a plan.

'Last time you brought humans together you nearly died,' Tiger pointed out.

'Well I'm not going to do that a second time,' I mused. 'I'm down to my last six lives I think, so I still need to do something and it has to be big.'

'Like getting stuck up a tree again,' Tiger teased.

'No, that's too—' I stopped, they had just given me an idea.

We were distracted by a low flying butterfly; Tom tried to swipe it at the same time as Tiger and their paws collided.

'Sorry,' Tom mumbled looking bashful.

'Well I don't know, Alfie, maybe it's enough that they are happier now. And they did say they'd speak to the neighbours. Maybe that's enough?'

'No, I don't think so.' I was a determined cat.

'But none of us have a clue what to do.' Snowball lay down and looked sad as she put her head in her paws. 'I'm worried they'll leave. I know they said things are looking better but they're still not happy. I really don't want to leave Edgar Road.' Snowball looked so sad, lying there, that my heart went out to her. I couldn't let that happen.

'I think I know what to do,' I exclaimed, remembering my earlier brainwave.

'Oh no, I'm not sure I want to know,' Tiger said, covering her ears with her paws. 'Knowing you it's going to be dangerous!'

'I want to know. Come on, Alfie, tell us,' Tom pushed.

'No, you are all going to have to wait and see. Tiger, tell Snowball how good I am at getting humans to do what I want.'

'He is, Snowball. He can convince any human of anything. He doesn't pull the fur over my eyes, but those humans fall for it every time.'

'I guess we've got nothing to lose.' Snowball sounded doubtful.

'And everything to gain,' I finished.

I felt a sense of purpose as we strutted home. I walked beside Snowball, whilst Tiger and Tom frolicked behind us. They definitely brought out the playful side in each other. We were almost at Snowball's gate, when Salmon jumped out on us. I had almost forgotten about him.

'Well, what do we have here,' he said, licking his lips ominously. 'You all look cosy together.' Snowball hissed, but I stood next to her protectively.

'Salmon, it's time you got lost. You and your nosey family. The Snells have nothing to hide and you might as well give up now.'

'What, because you tell us to?' He laughed nastily.

'No, because you're all making huge fools of yourselves. You're going to be the laughing stock of the street soon.' I sounded braver than I felt.

'You already are,' Tiger piped up from behind, reinforcing my confidence.

'Yes that petition didn't work, and we cats are thinking of getting a petition going against you,' Tom joked. He actually did have quite a good sense of humour now he was with Tiger.

'Cats can't write,' Salmon shot back.

'We'll use mouse blood to write it all over your yard,' Tom replied, but he didn't sound serious. I don't think he did anyway.

'You wouldn't dare?' Salmon looked afraid for the first ever time.

'Try us,' I challenged.

Salmon turned and ran back across the road.

'My hero,' Tiger said. 'Impressive.'

'You're my hero too,' Snowball whispered to me.

-CHAPTER-
Thirty-Six

Claire was disappointed. I think she believed that after the note they'd sent, Karen would be round, thanking them and perhaps inviting them for a cup of tea at the very least. She ranted a bit to Jonathan that the note Karen had sent back, which Claire referred to as a 'perfunctory' thank you, was far from satisfactory. So it was lucky that I had my plan. They needed a helping paw and luckily I was here to provide one.

I always thought that happiness was infectious. You know, contagious. I looked at all my families up and down the street, and even further afield, and realized how happy everyone was. Even us cats had nothing to worry about. We were all elated and I knew, if we could reach them then the Snells would catch it from us. We would literally infect them with happiness.

I breakfasted in Claire and Jonathan's happy house. Claire had let Jonathan give me tinned or fresh fish for days now, so I was pretty lucky. Something told me that when the baby came along they would be a bit distracted and I might not get the same attention, but if they were I had back-up. I refused to have any of my joy stamped on. Not even by Salmon who had taken to staring with hostile eyes at all us cats, although from a safe distance. He really was a coward after all.

He was extra-annoyed because Polly seemed to blame him for digging up her flowers. After my grand gesture, I'd forgotten about the slightly destroyed flower bed but Salmon had been caught lurking by her front garden, so when she jumped to that conclusion it suited me just fine.

★★★

'Alfie, you are probably only going to be gone for a few hours; you're acting as if this is your big farewell,' Tiger said, as I went to see her before implementing my plan.

'I am not. And anyway, if something goes wrong, then you'll wish you had treated me a bit more fondly.'

'Alfie, you're such a drama cat. You yourself said that there was no danger attached to this plan.'

'I know, but I would like everyone to appreciate what I am going to do.'

'But we don't know what it is!' I could see Tiger was exasperated, so I decided to confide in her and, for once, she actually listened carefully.

'Alfie, you are mad, after last time,' Tiger said. She didn't look every impressed.

'That's why it's so perfect, I've got experience in it now. But don't tell anyone,' I said. 'It's supposed to be a secret.' Tiger raised her whiskers, shook her head and smiled.

'You will never change. Be careful, Alfie, and hopefully you'll get what you want.'

It was afternoon before I headed into Snowball's house. I told her I would be there and she was in the kitchen waiting for me. She still had no idea what I was planning, so I thought I'd better tell her.

'Right, I'm going up the tree again,' I said.

'Why?' Snowball asked.

'Because then your family will go and get my family, they'll bond over the need to rescue me.' I was pretty confident with this plan. I had thought it out. My grand gesture hadn't worked exactly as I planned, but it had given me an idea. I was going to climb the tree again, pretend to be stuck (as this time

I would ensure my legs didn't seize up), and then Snowball would go and get help from our families. I could just picture the scene: that as they all talked about rescuing me, the Snells would realize what a good thing it was to have friends on the street, and whilst they were distracted I'd just climb down again. Of course, they'd all be so happy that I was safe that everyone would be friends. It was foolproof.

'What if Christopher just gets the ladder again?' Snowball asked.

'I thought of that. I'll go even higher so the grown-ups will have to get involved.' I remembered that the ladder only reached the branch I was on which wasn't that high, this time I would climb further.

'And you think that will work?'

'Yes, of course. Don't you?'

'What about your legs?'

'You worry too much. Right, wish me luck. And trust me, this will bond them, somehow, it really will.'

'Good luck. And, Alfie, either you're mad or a genius; I just hope it's the latter.'

Snowball followed me to the garden. I looked at the tree, feeling confident. I'd done it before I could it again and this time I was unencumbered by flowers so it would be easier. With confidence I started to climb. I began to enjoy myself. It was early evening and still pleasant; the sun was fairly warm, the sky blue. I saw some birds overhead and listened to them singing as I made my way, branch by branch into the tree.

I easily passed the place where I'd been when Christopher had rescued me and continued further on up. I could feel the wind in my fur as I carried on, brimming with determination with each branch I passed.

After a long, arduous climb I suddenly realized how tired I was, so I stopped to see if I was high enough. I got myself in position on the branch and looked down. 'Oh my goodness,' I thought, 'what has happened?' Snowball had shrunk – she was tiny! I looked again and saw just how high I was. I felt dizzy as the ground seemed to spin beneath me and I clung onto the branch for dear life. I cried out, but not as part of the plan; it was a cry of genuine terror as fear rushed through my fur. I had never been this high in my life and I was terrified. I thought about getting down, aborting the plan, but I couldn't move. It was as if I was literally paralysed by fear.

I couldn't see her face but I could see Snowball heading inside, yelling loudly. Thankfully she soon came out with Karen and Tim. Christopher and Daisy followed them and they all looked up at me. Unfortunately, I couldn't hear what they were saying; the wind seemed to take their words away and I was truly stuck in every sense of the word as they all stood below, looking up at me.

There was activity on the ground, as Daisy ran out back round the side of the house and disappeared. Making sure my back legs were securely on the branch, I put my paws over my eyes to see if that stopped me feeling sick, but then I couldn't bear not being able to see. I cemented myself to the branch wondering if I would have to stay here forever; would this be my new home?

After what felt like hours, Polly and Matt appeared in the garden. I fleetingly wondered where Claire and Jonathan were as I saw them all staring up at me, shaking their heads. Matt came to the bottom of the tree and shouted something up, but all I could hear was my name. I miaowed as loudly as I could but I couldn't be sure he heard me. I wanted to cry. This was not the amazingly straightforward plan I'd thought it was going to be.

No one moved from the garden now and although I couldn't see much, I did see Tim making a call. Matt was still trying to shout up to me, but the wind kept stealing his words so I couldn't hear him. I wished I was in his arms right now. Anyone's arms. I felt sick to my stomach as I huddled and clung on for dear life.

After about half an hour of being stuck to the branch, I heard the sirens from quite far away and instinctively knew what it was. Oh the indignity! My worst fear. Matt and Tim ran round to the front of the house, and after a while they came back with four firemen who looked up at me. I covered my eyes again. I would never live this down and if this didn't bring my families together then it would be the ultimate humiliation for nothing. They disappeared and then reappeared with a ladder that looked enormous. As they rested it against the tree, they started extending it before one man started climbing. Finally, I found myself face to face with a friendly looking fireman.

'OK, Alfie, you're safe now,' he said, as he reached for me and took me in his arms. He did have to literally peel me off the branch but as soon as I felt his arms around me I started to feel relief. I wouldn't have to live in the tree after all.

I closed my eyes as we made our way down the ladder. I was still feeling sick. He handed me to Polly who was crying.

'Thank you for rescuing him,' she said. 'Honestly, Alfie, sometimes I wonder about you, you could have fallen,' she chastised.

'Can I get you guys a cup of tea?' Karen offered the firemen.

'Nah, thanks, love, but we might have to put an actual fire

out!' he laughed. 'But take care of that cat, he's my first ever cat rescue,' the man who'd got me down said. 'And I've been in the brigade for over ten years.'

I had never been so embarrassed in my life.

Polly was still clutching me as we went round to the front of the house. Snowball followed and I could see she looked relieved, although I hadn't had the chance to talk to her yet.

The first thing I noticed was that the shiny red fire engine had attracted quite a crowd as most of the residents of Edgar Road stood around it — apart from the Goodwins of course, who were probably behind their curtains.

'My God, are you all right?' I heard panic in Claire's voice as she rushed across the street and up to Polly. 'We just got home and saw the fire engine. Is there a fire?'

'No, Claire, it was Alfie, he got stuck up a tree in the Snells' garden,' Matt explained, still looking shaken up. I felt bad that yet again that I had made my families worry about me but I told myself it was for the greater good. I noticed that my cat friends were also out, watching the goings on hidden beneath bushes. Tiger smiled at me and I tried to smile back, still feeling woozy from my adventure up the tree.

'He was so high,' Karen said. 'Poor little thing, none of us knew what to do so Tim called the fire brigade.'

'Are you all right?' Claire took me from Polly and cuddled me. I miaowed and snuggled into her; I was still feeling dizzy actually but so relieved to be out of the tree I almost didn't mind.

'Excuse me, it's Rob,' a man I recognized from the street said. 'I'm with the local paper and we'd love to do an article, it's not often that we get the old cat-up-a-tree story these days.'

Did he really have to rub it in?

The whole street seemed to be buzzing with excitement

as I was handed back to the fireman who rescued me and my picture was taken. For the paper! Could this get any worse?

'Right,' Jonathan announced to the Snells, after, it seemed, the whole neighbourhood had checked on me, taking the time to introduce themselves to the Snells who seemed shy but happy to shake hands and exchange words. 'Please come to our house so we can thank you with a drink at least.' I waited for the Snells to make their excuses but they nodded.

'That'd be lovely,' Tim said, to everyone's surprise, and we all happily made our way to our house.

Polly went to get the children whom she'd left with her neighbour, and I was pleased to see that it was noisy and full in our kitchen, just the way I liked it. Matt and Polly, Claire and Jonathan sat around the table with the Snells, Martha was asleep in her buggy and Henry was playing tiredly with some cars on the floor. Daisy and Christopher seemed animated by the situation and were chatting easily with everyone, and finally Tim decided to open up and tell everyone exactly what was going on. I saw him look at Karen as if asking for permission and she squeezed his hand and smiled.

I wanted to escape and see Snowball but Claire and Polly wouldn't let me out of their sight so instead, I listened to the familiar story that I had heard from Snowball as I rested. As Tim left no stone unturned, my humans looked horrified as they listened to their tale.

'It's terrible, but I wish we'd known,' Jonathan said. 'If only to get the Goodwins off your backs.'

'Yes, mate, sorry, we didn't handle it very well,' Tim explained.

'Yeah but after hearing all you've been through, no one can blame you,' Claire said, giving Karen's hand a reassuring squeeze.

I was still pretty shaken up from my ordeal, not to mention embarrassed. However, as I saw the happy faces in my kitchen, I tried to remember that I had got what I wanted. Well nearly, anyway.

I heard the cat flap and everyone turned to look as Snowball appeared.

'Snowball!' Daisy said. 'She's come to see if Alfie's OK.' She was gleeful.

Snowball miaowed and came over to my basket. She smiled at me and waved her tail and I knew she was happy as she curled down next to me.

'My goodness, that's the cutest thing I have ever seen,' Polly said.

'My God, Alfie's got himself a girlfriend,' Jonathan stated. Matt and Jonathan high-fived, the others all laughed and started chattering animatedly about us. Claire was pink with delight.

I looked at Snowball, she looked at me in understanding; humans could be so juvenile sometimes but I loved them anyway.

-EPILOGUE-

It was family day again, six months after I had been stuck up a tree. Oh how that story never got old, not with my cat friends, who thought it was hilarious. Tiger, after telling me she had warned me I wasn't good with trees, couldn't stop with her teasing, and the others joined in. Then, of course, it had made its way onto the front page of the local paper. Claire had even got the photo of me and the fireman framed so every day I had a reminder of my ultimate humiliation.

However, I was too happy at the fact that my plan worked to worry. What was a little embarrassment in the grand scheme of things?

It had taken a while to fully ensconce the Snells into our group but slowly they had learned to trust us. Tim, Matt and Jonathan watched football together, Karen was great company now she was happier, and they had been joining us on family days for a while now.

As it was a lovely day, we were going to have a picnic in the park, which was one of my favourite family days. Everyone was going to be there and I was beside myself with excitement. Before we left, Claire was making lots of food as I played around her feet, Jonathan was getting hot and bothered as he tried to find picnic blankets and folding chairs – which of course were where they always were. And baby Summer, who had arrived over a month ago, was curled up in her Moses basket, sleeping. I could barely take my eyes off her, she was so beautiful, and Claire teased that I was her bodyguard. Luckily, so far, that was easy, as all she did was eat and sleep – a bit like

Tiger when I first met her, actually.

I loved all my human children but when they had brought Summer home from hospital, I had fallen in love with her immediately. She was my new sister and I would do anything to make sure she was looked after. She already lived up to her name. As soon as she entered the house, it was sunny all the time. Even when she woke up throughout the night, no one moaned and Claire and Jonathan were happier than I had ever seen them.

It wasn't long before Polly and Matt called round, both children ensconced in the stroller, carrying even more food and chairs.

We waited by the front gate and Jonathan, with Summer strapped to his chest, went to get the Snells. Karen opened the door, smiling shyly, shouted for the others and joined us on the pavement. I looked at Snowball and grinned. We both stopped and looked and saw the Goodwins twitching their curtains across the road. All our humans waved over at them, and they waved back. The Goodwins weren't our friends but they had accepted the Snells at last, especially as they had gone to a couple of their Neighbourhood Watch meetings and taken homemade cake with them.

Snowball smiled at me as we set off for the park.

Jonathan and Matt were arranging blankets when Franceska and Tomasz and the boys arrived. Aleksy was clutching his precious football, I was pleased to see.

'Hey, shall we play football while they set up lunch?' Christopher asked.

So much had changed. Not only did we have Summer now but the Snells were far happier. Tim had got a job and loved going to work again. Karen had managed to cut back on her hours so she wasn't so tired. Polly had taken Daisy to see a model agency because she'd finished her exams and she was going to try out for a few jobs in the school holidays before she went back to do A-levels, and Christopher had started playing football at his school and was so good he was something of a star.

And Snowball and I were friends. Proper friends, close friends, although so far it hadn't become anything more. I didn't want to push her, so I had treaded carefully; things were changing but I could tell she needed more time. However, I was feeling optimistic that today was the day that I would make the breakthrough I'd been planning for months.

And it all started with me getting stuck up a tree.

'Yeah!' Aleksy shouted and he and Christopher took the ball to the centre of the park. Little Tomasz bounded after them, amid shouts from his father not to lose the ball this time. Henry ran as fast as he could to join in but when the boys started kicking the ball he hung back, nervously. I joined him, as did Snowball. We watched as Christopher showed off some impressive ball skills to an utterly amazed Aleksy.

Matt, Jonathan and Tim came over.

'Wow, he's so good,' Matt said.

'He's become the star at school, not that he likes us to acknowledge that,' Tim said with pride.

'Let's join them,' Jonathan suggested. They all bounded onto the small area, kicking the ball and although Christopher was clearly the only person who could play, they were all having fun.

'Fun has re-entered our lives, Alfie, thanks to you,' Snowball said as if reading my mind.

'And you know I did it for you,' I replied as I nuzzled her neck.

'Come on, boys, lunch,' Franceska called a little while later, and they all made their way over, Matt carrying Henry. The children sat together on one blanket, the adults on another. Although Daisy sat with the adults, Chris was next to his biggest fan, Aleksy. Aleksy adored him, and I was so happy to see how great Christopher was with him; like a big brother almost.

I lay down and basked in the sun with Snowball by my side as my families chatted with hers as they feasted on the lovely food everyone had brought; I looked forward to the leftovers later.

'It seems so strange to think so much has changed this year,' Franceska said. She often became reflective when we all got together. Big Tomasz put his arm around her.

'We've been through the mill but seem to have come out the other side,' Tim said.

'I'll drink to that,' Jonathan said and the men clinked their beer bottles.

'Jonathan, do you remember when you thought they might be like Batman, but a whole family of crime fighters,' Matt laughed.

'Cheers for reminding us, Matt, it was only a theory,' Jonathan laughed.

'Excuse my husband, he's almost as mad as the Goodwins sometimes.' Claire stroked Jonathan's arm affectionately as Franceska cuddled a sleeping Summer.

'It seems the cakes have worked, they're civil to us now,' Karen said.

'Yes – although remember it's a fine line. You don't want to encourage them too much or they'll be popping round all the time.'

'Good point, we'll have to make sure we draw all the curtains at least once a week,' Tim joked.

As glasses chinked and more drinks were poured, Snowball

and I left our families and headed to the flower beds.

'Looking back, your plan, as fragile as it seemed, worked,' she said.

'And I got rescued by a fireman for you guys.' I still expected praise and even sympathy for it all these months later, I had to be honest.

'You're right, and thank you. It's like a happy ending all round.' Snowball stretched out her body and yawned. A combination of sun and happiness was enough to make any cat tired.

'Well, not quite,' I said meaningfully. 'It's time for me to stop pussy-footing around,' I declared.

'When have you ever pussy-footed, Alfie?' she teased.

'OK, well maybe I haven't but you know … well … you obviously know what I am trying to say, don't you?' I felt exposed, embarrassed and unsure.

'Perhaps, you need to spell it out,' Snowball replied, looking deep into my eyes and making my legs turn to jelly.

'You are the most infuriating cat I've ever met. Even more so than Tiger. But you are also the most beautiful, and you make me feel alive, like I'm a better cat when I am around you. I need to know you feel the same.'

'Oh, Alfie, of course I feel the same. No one has ever got stuck up a tree twice, ripped up flower beds or been rescued by a fireman for me. And even without all that, I think you are a wonderful, handsome cat and I couldn't imagine my life without you now.' I happily nuzzled her neck, as Aleksy came running over.

'Alfie!' he shouted as the others joined him. 'Snowball. I think they are in love!' he announced.

Aleksy was holding his brother's hand. Daisy was standing close to Christopher. Martha and Henry were holding onto the railings and peering at us. Jonathan had his arm around Claire who was carrying Summer. Polly and Matt were holding hands and Tim had his arm around Karen's waist. Snowball and I were pressed together looking at all the humans who loved each other and loved us too.

I felt as if I could actually see the love that surrounded me and as I looked at the faces of those that made my up all my families, I smiled the broadest smile a cat could. I had loved and lost and loved some more – but through all the happiness and sadness, there was one thing that I would never doubt. This doorstep cat was the luckiest cat in the world.

One ordinary neighbourhood.
One extraordinary cat.

Read the *Sunday Times* bestseller and find out
how it all started. The tale of one little grey cat
and his journey to become a Doorstep Cat.